"The name is Winter Wesson," he said, with a thick British accent. "May I ask your name?"

"Eve Bloom, sorry, Blair." Eve cleared her throat. "I am recently divorced and still getting used to the name change."

"Interesting," he frowned. "I must read more about divorce customs in these times. There is no divorce in my time."

Eve rolled her eyes. "Okay, enough. If you want to stay here, please stay in the owner's suite. It's at the back of the building. And do not make any purchases with the great house money. Call the head of the board of trustees, Stuart Smithson, and he will happily work out an income for you. The trustees exist to serve the Wesson heirs."

"I won't be staying long enough for that, not this time," Winter said. "I was so excited the last time I was here that I went a little overboard. All of this is strange and yet exhilarating. The changes in this country, in the world, are mind-boggling."

Eve smiled. "Oh, they are?"

"If you went forward three hundred years, you would say the same thing, Eve Blair," Winter leaned forward, his eyes twinkling. "I find that the longer I look at you, the more exhilarated I feel."

WINTER'S EVE

BRENDA BARRETT

WINTER'S EVE
A Jamaica Treasures Book/November 2024
Published by Jamaica Treasures
Manchester, Jamaica

This is a work of fiction. Names, characters, places, and incidents are either the product of the author's imagination or are used fictitiously. Any resemblance to an actual person or persons, living or dead, events, or locales is entirely coincidental.

No part of this book may be reproduced or transmitted in any form or by any means, electronic or mechanical, including photocopying, recording, or by any information storage and retrieval system, without permission in writing from the Publisher, except where permitted by law.

ISBN 978-976-97430-0-7

ALSO BY BRENDA BARRETT

FULL CIRCLE
NEW BEGINNINGS
THE PREACHER AND THE PROSTITUTE
AFTER THE END
THE EMPTY HAMMOCK
THE PULL OF FREEDOM
REBOUND SERIES
THREE RIVERS SERIES
NEW SONG SERIES
BANCROFT SERIES
MAGNOLIA SISTERS SERIES
SCARLETT SERIES
WILEY BROTHERS SERIES
PRYCE SISTERS SERIES
THE JACKSONS SERIES
CRIMSON HILL SERIES
SPICE AND STONE SERIES
RIDGEVIEW SERIES

ABOUT THE AUTHOR

Brenda Barrett is an award-winning and bestselling author who has a passion for writing real Jamaican romances.

When she's not weaving words that transport readers to exotic locales, you can find her nurturing her green thumb in the garden or doting on her beloved cats.

With an infectious zest for life, this author brings a unique perspective to her writing that is both relatable and thought-provoking.

Don't be surprised if you find yourself lost in the pages of her latest work, as she seamlessly blends romance with some drama, mystery, and suspense, or even sci-fi, leaving readers wanting more.

You can connect with Brenda online at:
Brenalbar.com
Facebook.com/AuthorBrendaBarrett

Chapter One

It was the phone that woke her up. The incessant rings would not let up, and Eve felt like she had just gotten into bed. The great house had just hosted a party. They had done thousands of them, but it had been personal this time. Stuart Smithson, the head of the board of trustees, was celebrating his 50th birthday, and he had chosen this Wesson property to have the party.

Of course, as the property manager, Eve wanted everything to be perfect. Over the last few days, she had run the staff and herself ragged; a successful party would reflect greatly on her management skills, especially since she had slacked off for a couple of months while going through her divorce.

She needed this job now more than ever. Thankfully, Stuart and his guests had been impressed.

She had stuck around until the last guest had left the property and the clean-up crew had finished restoring the place to its former glory. Then she had climbed into bed, practically dead on her feet.

When she slept over by the great house, she usually stayed in what was previously known as the counting house. The two-bedroom, one-bathroom cottage had been converted into a living area in the late 1800s. Back then, people would not count money in their homes; it was considered bad luck. And so, they had a counting house separate from the main house. It was renovated and modernized with internal plumbing, but it kept the old charm.

She put the pillow over her ears and waited for the phone to stop ringing, but it started again. She searched for it blindly on the side table, knocking over her a water bottle and pushing her car keys onto the ground.

She answered without opening her eyes. She didn't know if they could be opened; they felt gritty and unrested.

"Good morning," she croaked.

"It's afternoon," Stuart's said. "Can we meet for lunch? I've been hearing the most extraordinary things from Maud. I just saw a video of a dead ringer for Winter Wesson. I can't quite believe what I am seeing. Maud said you spoke to this fellow. I would love to hear everything you discussed and what transpired between you. Who on earth is he?"

Eve groaned. Everything? Stuart didn't need to know that.

"Er, I'll be there in fifteen minutes," she said huskily.

She should have known Stuart would be up and gossiping with Maud. He and Maud loved conspiracies and intrigue where there was none.

He would have stayed at the back of the great house. The owner's suite was added in the early 1900s by one of the Wessons who occupied the place then. The new addition blended seamlessly with the rest of the house. They even used the same wild orange board flooring and continued with the aesthetics from the colonial era.

She flung the pillow from over her head and looked around her suite. The décor was timeless and could fit in any era: dark hardwood floors, neutral white walls, and white linen drapes framed the tall windows. The four-poster bed made from mahogany dominated the room, and the antique side tables and writing desk were meticulously preserved.

The atmosphere of the place screamed opulence and history. She usually took a moment after waking up to pull the curtains and step out onto her patio to inhale the pure air of the countryside and admire the gardens immediately below. The blue and white African lilies were making a showy appearance at this time of year. Or she would look farther into the landscape where rolling hills converged to the sea.

Crimson Hill Great House had quite a view. She couldn't admire much this morning; she didn't even pull the curtains; she stumbled to the ensuite bathroom. Thankfully, it had modern amenities such as a shower, a separate clawfoot tub, and hot and cold water. She would choose the cold water and stand in the shower, allowing the water to reinvigorate her. That was one advantage of having short hair, even though her mother had whined and complained about it. She had chopped her hair off after the divorce and wore it in a short, curly cap.

In her opinion, it made her look more sophisticated, and it was easy to care for. Unfortunately, the shorter style took years off her face; though she was twenty-nine, she looked like a teenager.

When they first met, the Winter Wesson look-alike had called her 'but a girl'. Eve had tried so hard to forget the events from last summer, but apparently, she wouldn't have the luxury of doing so since Stuart wanted a blow-by-blow account about her encounter with Winter Wesson.

"Who are you?" she remembered demanding of the stranger Maud had dragged into her office with a triumphant smile. The man looked like the identical twin of Winter Wesson whose portrait hung in the ballroom and library they had the same vivid green eyes, olive-toned skin, and black overlong hair.

His left eyebrow had the same gap as the portrait as if it were parted by a thin scar. He was wearing the same clothing as in the picture, minus the jacket. He wore a loose, comfortable-fit shirt with ruffled cuffs and a high collar, a green silk waistcoat, knee-length breeches, stockings, and leather shoes with low heels.

She would have laughed if she weren't so shocked; he looked authentic. The only thing missing was the tricorn hat, like the one in the portrait and those she had seen in the movie, Pirates of the Caribbean.

"He is Winter Wesson," Maud answered for the man.

He folded his hands and looked at her with his head cocked to the side, an air of irreverence to him like he found her question funny.

"She is but a girl, Maud. Are you sure she is the one in charge?"

Maud had cackled. "She is in charge, and she accused me and Willie of running up her expenses when you came last year. Please let her know that you were the one who did it."

"I am the one who ran up the expenses," he said, sitting before her desk and looking at her nonchalantly. You are a pretty girl with fabulous bone structure."

Eve had been shocked into silence, and then she opened her mouth. "I am not a girl. I am the property manager for this place."

"Pardon me," he chuckled.

"We have protocols for doing things; you are obviously a Wesson," Eve sputtered. "You should contact the board of trustees, let them know who you are, and proceed accordingly. It's inappropriate to bypass established procedures, regardless of your family name. You cannot just show up at the great house, sleep in our showrooms, and make outlandish orders on my budget!"

He chuckled and leaned back in his chair. "I wonder which of my descendants was responsible for a board of trustees."

"You were," Maud said, "you wanted to preserve the history of the place for generations to come, and you wanted to ensure that your children's children would benefit from your legacy."

Eve groaned. "Maud, leave us. I want to speak with this man privately."

"The name is Winter Wesson," he said, with a thick British accent. "May I ask your name?"

"Eve Bloom, sorry, Blair." Eve cleared her throat. "I am recently divorced and still getting used to the name change."

"Interesting," he frowned. "I must read more about divorce customs in these times. There is no divorce in my time."

Eve rolled her eyes. "Okay, enough. If you want to stay here, please stay in the owner's suite. It's at the back of the building. And do not make any purchases with the great house money. Call the head of the board of trustees, Stuart Smithson, and he will happily work out an income for you. The trustees exist to serve the Wesson heirs."

"I won't be staying long enough for that, not this time," Winter said. "I was so excited the last time I was here that I went a little overboard. All of this is strange and yet exhilarating. The changes in this country, in the world, are mind-boggling."

Eve smiled. "Oh, they are?"

"If you went forward three hundred years, you would say the same thing, Eve Blair," Winter leaned forward, his eyes twinkling. "I find that the longer I look at you, the more exhilarated I feel."

"Get out of my office," Eve growled, "and please put the costumes back in the closet."

He got up.

"And ask Maud to prepare the owner's suite for you. There should be no sleeping in the main house."

He laughed. "Another noteworthy change is that women are bossy in this century. I quite like it."

Chapter Two

Eve felt remorseful for being grumpy with Fake Winter. The man was obviously indulging in a fantasy within his ancestor's home, whom he closely resembled. If today hadn't been so busy, she would have responded more calmly. They could have even discussed how his cosplaying of Winter Wesson could benefit their great house tours. They could even feature him in their brochures and website.

She was beginning to feel excited about the prospect. She wondered about his profession, how long he intended to stay at the Great House, and how much it would cost them for his services.

The Great House was on track to make record profits this year, and she could afford some extras. Unfortunately, she was pressed for time and couldn't have a lengthy meeting with him to discuss the details. It was four o'clock, and she had promised her mother to attend her law firm's annual fundraiser gala at six.

She needed to shop for something to wear; all her finery was still packed in boxes in her new apartment, awaiting unpacking. Besides, she wanted to make a good impression. She had to get her nails done, and it would take her at least half an hour to apply her makeup to look like she had just stepped off a magazine cover.

This was important; it was the first time she would see her ex-husband face-to-face after their divorce. It was a divorce she had not wanted, but he had insisted on because he had found his one true love and didn't want to cheat on her.

Eve sighed; that familiar pang in her chest resurfaced whenever she thought about it. And, of course, the image of David's earnest face when he had declared, "I don't love you, Eve. I never did. I married you because your religious parents required us to get married instead of just moving in together like I had wanted.

"And since I work in your mother's firm and didn't want to get fired, I just went along with it. None of this would have happened if we had just moved in together. I would be free to leave whenever I found my true love; you were just a stopgap until I found her."

Eve still remembered the conversation as vividly as if it had happened just hours ago. Why was it still so fresh? Time was supposed to heal her wounds. What on earth was time doing?

Her wound was still fresh. It hadn't even scabbed over.

David had been so eager to get her out of his life that he moved out of their marital home and in with his girlfriend, fellow lawyer, Tiffany Bell, who also worked at the law firm and whom she suspected he was cheating with long before his little speech.

She had tried to punish him by not granting him the divorce he wanted. She refused to let go of the surname Bloom and ignored all attempts by David to divorce her before the two years of living separately, as laid out by the law.

She had somehow thought that he would come to his senses, get tired of Tiffany, and return to her, but that didn't happen.

He couriered divorce papers to her as soon as it was legally possible. Her mother had urged her to sign them.

"Sign them, Eve. The man clearly does not want you. You need to move on."

"Why can't you fire him?" Eve had asked passionately. "And her too."

"Because he is a junior partner and one of the highest earners this year, and Tiffany has been our only real estate lawyer since Evan left. Honey, it's business. We signed contracts. It would be easier for you to divorce him than me."

Eve had fumed, but her mother had held firm. "What I can do for you is forbid Gavin from representing David in the divorce and ask him to represent you instead. Trust me, Gavin is the best family law attorney in this section of Jamaica; David will be uncomfortable."

She didn't want him uncomfortable; she wanted him to quake in his boots. So, Eve had told Gavin to do his worst. Gavin had grinned with glee. "That's what I do. When I am done with him, he will cry in the lobby every day. He'll be sorry he messed with you."

"Aren't you two golfing buddies?" Eve had asked Gavin.

"Yes," Gavin nodded, "but I don't mix business with pleasure."

She had fought David tooth and nail for everything, trying to be as difficult as possible. Her dad had given her the house as a wedding present, and David had wanted it.

It was the one thing he wanted: to be close to his family

and the golf club. Gavin had made sure that he didn't get it.

She had gotten the marital home and the mutual bank account, but she had lost her self-esteem and sense of self-worth. They had been obliterated with the declaration that she was just a stopgap. After two years of marriage where she thought she had an exemplary relationship and that her husband loved her, only to hear that she had been a stopgap, a temporary way of dealing with a problem or satisfying a need.

Goodness gracious, she hated the word.

And now, here she was, one year later, trying to pretend that she was whole again and could face him at the firm's fundraiser with no bitterness. This was the first in two years that they would be in the same room. When David had just moved out and in with Tiffany, their friends and family had been forced to pick sides, choosing who to invite to functions so that they wouldn't meet. Eve had been close to the Bloom family, so that had been a blow. She had enjoyed being an aunt to David's six nieces and nephews from his three siblings. Now, those relationships were lost. That was one of the things that hurt the most: when you divorce a person, you divorce their whole family. She had loved the Bloom family dynamic.

Her younger sister Evita lived in France, and they only saw each other yearly at Christmas, if that. Her sister could not travel last year because she was heavily pregnant.

Her parents were busy people with full lives. Her mother was a criminal attorney with her own practice, and her father was a real estate dealer with his own firm. The Blairs had never experienced the bustling family life of the Blooms.

David's two sisters, a brother, and their spouses lived within walking distance of each other. She had fallen in love with the family as much as she had fallen for David, and now, just like that, all of it was over. She had thought it would last forever. Maybe she was just as delusional as Fake Winter Wesson.

She packed her things in her briefcase, grabbed her laptop bag, and headed out. Her office was a suite of rooms on the right wing of the great house. It was an addition, like the owner's suite. In the past, it was used as a two-bedroom apartment with its own bathroom. It had its own entrance, garden, and a small side gate to keep away visitors. It was on the same path as the owner's suite and counting house, but this section of the house was not open for tours or functions. It was too modernized to fit in with the narrative, and whoever stayed on that side could enjoy some privacy without bumping into tourists.

The Wesson, who had built it in the late 1800s, had been careful to make the exterior similar to the main house. She exited the office, locking the door behind her. Usually, her administrative assistant, Rosette, would stay until five, but Rosette was on maternity leave.

Maud entered the side gate with a covered tray, smiling like the cat that got the canary.

"What's that?" Eve asked.

"Oh, this is lunch for Mr. Wesson," Maud said. "He hasn't eaten a thing all day; he had Craig showing him how to use the internet."

Eve widened her eyes. "Craig, our newest tour guide?"

"Yes," Maud nodded.

"So, who is doing tours if he is off helping Fake Winter Wesson?"

Maud chuckled. "Nia is picking up the slack."

"And who is manning the shop if you are here catering to him?" Eve raised her eyebrows.

"Anastasia," Maud said guiltily.

"The volunteer!" Eve shook her head. "Maud…"

"Okay, okay, I should get back," Maud said. "Can you take this to him?"

"Me?" Eve frowned. "Maud, I am not Fake Winter Wesson's servant. Besides, I have an event…"

She changed her mind as soon as she said it. The Great House could use the man's services. Didn't she just have that thought a moment ago?

"Okay, I'll do it," Eve said.

Maud smiled. "Good. It will help you get to know him."

"Not today," Eve took the tray from Maud. "This smells good. What did you prepare for him?"

"He said he wanted something spicy, so I did some bammies and Escovitch fish with extra pepper. For an Englishman from the seventeen hundreds, he certainly likes spicy food," Maud chuckled.

Eve chuckled. "His modern tastes do give him away. Did you hear what he said about me having a fabulous bone structure? A white man from the seventeen hundreds thinking that a black woman is pretty is weird."

"Not really," Maud replied. "They liked black women alright. White women were not willing to come here to the colonies, so they took the slave women as bed partners.

"Some of them even had long-standing relationships with the black women they were attracted to. I am sure some women were also attracted to them, at the very least, because they had the power to make their lives easier. And not to forget that even though some of them had their wives here, mixed race babies were born quite frequently in the slave cabins."

"One thing about you, Maud, you know your history," Eve grinned.

"I do," Maud said. "And that's why I know Winter Wesson

is different; his whole family is different. His family never believed in slavery. How many families of that era can say that? Very few, I tell you. But I can understand why.

"Winter's mother was half Portuguese and half Native Brazilian. I forgot her tribe name. His father was the second son of a duke. Before his brother died, he was an adventurer. He sailed to Brazil at the start of the gold rush and established himself there.

"He married the Brazilian, established his home, and then had to move back to England with his wife when his brother and father died.

"Winter's mother was hated in England; they treated her shabbily because of her dark skin. So I am sure she brought up her boys to be anti-racist."

"Maud, that's fascinating, but I must leave shortly if I am going to make it to my mother's event."

"Okay," Maud nodded. "I just wanted you to know that he is not the typical colonial blowhard. He is surprisingly open-minded, learns fast, and adjusts easily. He likes you, so give him a chance."

Eve chuckled. "No, thank you. I am not interested in Fake Winter Wesson and his time travel tales."

"You say that now," Maud muttered.

Eve pretended to ignore her and headed to the owner's suite. Craig and Fake Winter were bent over the laptop.

"I can't believe this," Winter kept muttering.

"What can't you believe?" Eve asked.

"St. John, St. George, St. David, and St. Dorothy are missing from your present map, and this parish is no longer St. James," Winter looked up at her. "I expected changes, but your map is vastly different from ours even the shape of the island is subtly different."

"I didn't know there was a St. David," Eve widened her

eyes. "Imagine that."

"I didn't know we were once part of St. James," Craig said. "According to this internet page, Trelawny was formed in 1770 and named after the then-governor William Trelawny.

"Never heard of him," Winter said. "That won't happen until fifty years my time!"

"I knew that; it was one of those random facts we studied for the Schools Challenge Quiz; I was on my high school team," Eve said. "Jamaica once had 22 parishes; now we have 14. It's disconcerting to hear that one of them was David. I don't like the word saint in front of David," Eve smirked.

"Why is that so, Miss Blair?" Winter looked at her interestedly.

"Because my ex-husband's name is David," Eve said, "and the devil would be a more apt description than saint. Devil David, I like the sound of that."

Craig snickered.

Eve looked at him, "I'll need to speak with you tomorrow, Craig. Shouldn't you be somewhere else?"

Craig sobered up and nodded. "Yes, Miss Eve. I should go, I have the tour after this. Do you remember how to turn off the computer, Winter?"

"I do," Winter nodded.

"I'll take the cord for you later so you can charge it, and do some more browsing."

"Thank you, Craig," Winter nodded. "You have been of great help."

Eve placed the container that Maud had sent over in front of him. "This is compliments of Maud."

"She is a delightful woman," Winter said gratefully. "I will somehow find a way to reward her for her excellent hospitality. Perhaps I will leave a pouch of gold coins under the carriage house floorboards for her to find."

"A pouch of gold? You are quite creative," Eve laughed. "I wish I could stay and chat with you, but I have a gala to attend, and I will need time to make myself beautiful."

"You are already beautiful," Winter said.

Eve looked at him, stunned. He meant it; he looked at her like she was the most captivating person he had ever seen. His gaze was filled with genuine admiration and affection.

Eve felt a flutter in her stomach, surprised by the intensity of her reaction to his words. She had not entertained any sort of attraction with the opposite sex for so long that she was actually feeling grateful for his simple compliment. She found herself momentarily lost in his gaze, forgetting about the gala and any other distractions.

At that moment, the two of them shared a connection that felt deeper than mere words could convey. She tore her gaze from Winter's and glanced at her watch.

"I really must be going," she said. "Let's discuss this again tomorrow. You know where my office is. I'll be there from nine o'clock."

Winter nodded. "Of course. Enjoy the gala, Eve. And know that you will always be beautiful in my eyes."

Chapter Three

The gala was at a hotel ballroom, and Eve was half an hour late. Her carefully planned entrance had flopped dramatically.

The little black dress she had picked up off the rack in a hurry fit her perfectly, as if it were made for her and was just waiting for her to retrieve it from the store. Her curls had never behaved better. It was her makeup that had given her the problem. She had run late after pondering whether she should go with a less-is-more approach or go full-face.

She blamed Fake Winter for this. The man had unsettled her with his declaration that she will always be beautiful in his eyes.

Who tells a total stranger that? Or looked at her so intensely that her skin burned almost two hours later. She had opted for basic makeup.

Her skin was clear and blemish-free, her eyes were bright and clear, and her lips were pink all on their own. She was the picture of health without enhancements. And besides, she had stopped thinking about trying to impress David; Fake Winter was front and center in all her thoughts.

"Darling," her mother greeted her at the door, "you look lovely!"

"Thanks, Mom. So do you," Eve smiled. Her mother was in a midnight blue ball gown, her long sister locks curled and in an elegant updo, and a few tendrils were out and hitting her at the waist.

"So, he is here," her mother pulled her aside. "And he is engaged. He gave Tiffany a big old rock; it's obscene and looks like costume jewelry if you ask me."

Eve chuckled. "I love it when you are catty about David."

"I wish you had brought someone," her mother said fretfully.

"I am fine, Mom, honest," Eve said. And she really meant it. She didn't know how it was possible, but one intense look from Fake Winter and a declaration that she was beautiful in his eyes had raised her self-confidence to heights it had never been before.

Her mother looked at her curiously. "I believe you. So, who is the new guy, and when can we meet him?"

Eve laughed. "Does there have to be a new guy?"

"No, but there is a look about you; I like it, keep it up. I have to go and greet others, but I expect to hear everything about him."

Eve chuckled and then looked around. There were quite a few people to mingle with seeing that she had grown up with most of them. She entered the fray. It wasn't long before she spotted David.

He was standing with Tiffany, his hand around her bare back. They were talking to a group. Tiffany was in a green dress, her long hair in a half-up, half-down hairstyle.

She looked around and saw Eve first and widened her eyes. She had beautiful hazel eyes, which was her best feature; she wasn't traditionally pretty; her jaw was sharply defined, and her mouth a bit too wide, but she was fascinating to look at. She reminded Eve of a cat.

Tiffany searched the crowd to see if she had a date, and when she saw that she didn't, she gave her a pitiful half-smile.

At least, that's how Eve interpreted it.

She wished her mother had been petty enough to fire them. Eve watched as Tiffany whispered to David, and he turned and looked at her.

They had a whisper fest, and then he walked over. He had a drink in hand. She knew from personal experience that he was just holding the glass for show.

He was tall and slim, with coffee-colored skin, a straight-as-an-arrow nose, generous kissable lips, and dark brown eyes the color of rich mahogany. He was cleanly shaven, even the hair on his head. He was the definition of tall, dark, and handsome—a candidate for the runways in Paris or the cover of a gentleman's magazine.

She remembered when she had first seen him. She had visited her mother at the office; he was the new hire to replace one of the six lawyers who had left. He was fresh out of law school and had been grateful for the opportunity to work with Veronica Blair. Her mother was famous for representing high-profile clients.

Their eyes had met in the lobby. He didn't know that she was Veronica's daughter at the time. He had introduced himself and told her why he was there.

She had developed a crush almost instantly. She had thought it was love at first sight, but seeing the stars she had in her eyes for him and an over-exuberant crush, David had probably thought it was a good career move to date Veronica's naïve daughter.

A year later, they were married on her twenty-fourth birthday. They had managed to make it two years together. A lousy two years. And she had made him wait two years for the divorce, which had been finalized on her birthday.

This year, on her twenty-ninth birthday, she had both her marriage and divorce to celebrate.

Someone had stopped him on his way to her. She turned away. Her mother was right; she should have brought someone.

"Eve," he said behind her.

Eve inhaled and then spun around, "Devil David."

He chuckled. "It's nice to see you."

Eve nodded. "Well… I don't want to lie and say likewise."

"I see there is still animosity there," David sighed. "Believe it or not, I never wanted to hurt you. I just couldn't think of a pain-free way to tell you the truth. And believe me, I understand your reluctance to speak to me. I hoped that time would have tempered your bitter feelings, but I can't blame you for holding onto them. I know apologies might not mean much now, but I truly am sorry for how things turned out between us."

That was a mouthful of insincere drivel. Eve contemplated telling him to shove it, but instead, she inhaled raggedly.

"Well, apology accepted."

What else was there to say? She wanted to yell, screech, and act like a mad woman; how dare you call me a stopgap! You cretin!

There was a moment of silence between them while Eve lovingly contemplated all the choice words she could call him.

She dared not open her mouth; she couldn't make small

talk, no, she couldn't. She struggled to find the right thing to say without sounding like a bitter, rejected ex-wife.

And then it registered. She wasn't really mad at him anymore. She was facing David, and the thought that kept coming to mind was how happy she was that they didn't have children together.

Could you imagine if they had procreated, and she had to hear about him and Tiffany? She managed a smile; there were small mercies.

"I hear congratulations are in order for you and Tiffany," she broke the awkward pause.

He nodded. "Yes, thank you."

"Well, now that the post-divorce meeting is over," Eve said, "we can mingle in peace."

David smiled. "You are, as usual, refreshingly blunt."

"Refreshingly blunt?"

He was gearing up to ask her something. When had her bluntness ever been refreshing?

"I heard you are selling the house."

And there it was.

Eve nodded. "I am considering selling it. I haven't made up my mind one way or another."

"Would you consider selling it to me?" David asked. "It's at an ideal location, close to my family and golf."

Eve resisted the urge to sneer. You should have thought of that before you left me. But she said out loud, "I'll let you know."

She deliberately caught the eye of one of her mother's chattier colleagues, Morgan Tracy.

He waved her over. He knew she would need saving from David.

"Excuse me," Eve said curtly. At least she didn't add, you evil user. He only apologized and acted humble because he wanted the house.

Just like he had only married her because she was his boss's daughter. David Bloom was a user. And she had spent way too much time over the last two years putting herself down for such a man. Maybe there was space for one who told her she was beautiful and meant it.

Chapter Four

Winter spent all evening on the Internet. He had encountered it before on his first visit to the future, and he had marveled at it then. There had seemed to be information about everything at his fingertips when he had seen it first.

He had read the history of Jamaica and England. He had seen the advancements in the world in videos and pictures. He was awestruck, not only by the information but also by the way it was conveyed. So why was it that he couldn't find information on Murdock Bartholomew in 1720?

He got varied descriptions of the golden era of piracy, 1718-1720, but no concrete information on the pirate he sought.

He had to admit it was heartening to see that some of the most notorious ones, like Calico Jack and Charles Vane, died that year, but there was no word of Murdock Bartholomew.

Was it wishful thinking of him to hope that he was one of the forty-one pirates that were hanged in 1720? There were so many that their names weren't recorded.

And how was he even to trust the calendar discrepancies with the way time was measured in this century versus the eighteenth century?

He knew firsthand that the dates did not line up. For him, the year started in March; in this century, it was January.

In his time, September was the seventh month, October the eighth, November the ninth, December the tenth, January the eleventh, and February the last month of the year.

In this century, September was the ninth month. It still baffled him why the Latin word "septem," which meant seven, was now accepted as the ninth month. Shouldn't the names reflect the order of the months?

The Julian and Gregorian differences in calendars proved to be a challenge for him when reading the historical accounts. Only a few sources differentiated between the Old Style Year and the New Style Year, not to mention the mixing up of the names for the month.

He didn't have the patience to scan through reams of data about calendars. He wanted to know where Murdock was in September 1720 so that he could find his brother, Wesley, and he needed a precise date and time.

This century was not proving to be as forthcoming with answers as he had excitedly told Walker.

He had reassured Winter that he would not only rescue Wesley from Murdock, but they could ambush him, armed with the foreknowledge of this century, and take him down once and for all.

How wrong he was.

He pushed away from the table and started pacing in frustration. Why hadn't he written it down?

None of the diaries he had written covered the years 1720 or beyond. Maud had supplied him with all of his diaries.

Why had he stopped writing, or were they destroyed? He paced the veranda.

He feared for Wesley's life; his brother was not used to the rough and tumble of a pirate's world. He would be terrified. He had just finished his schooling at Eton, where he would have learned Greek, Latin, History, and Music.

Somehow, he didn't think those lessons would come in handy with Murdock and his men. His poor brother would be traumatized.

His father had wanted to send Wesley to Brazil to toughen up, where he would work with their grandfather, Alvaro Caldeiro, to learn the family business. But Wesley had made a detour to Jamaica to visit him and Walker.

If their mother had been alive, this would surely have finished her off; Wesley had been her cherished child, her company, the final one to leave the nest.

Unfortunately, she had passed away from influenza three years prior. The only good thing about Wesley's capture was that she wouldn't hear about this.

It would be her dreaded nightmare coming to life. The pirate activity was why she hadn't visited her precious homeland, Brazil, for years.

On her first visit to England, she didn't like the journey by sea and had a nerve-wracking time on the ship. Though she hated England with a passion, she stayed because she hated sailing even more.

She had suffered greatly under the racism shown to her by the ton. She had been a pariah in their social circles because her skin was too dark; she had more melanin than a society obsessed with an English rose complexion had been comfortable with, and her accent was too foreign, though she had spoken perfect English.

She became the reclusive duchess, refusing to participate

in any social gatherings, preferring to putter about in her gardens at Wesson House and ride her horses.

Winter was tempted to read up on his family history. He had avoided doing so on the two previous visits. What would be the point?

But he may have to do so now. He wanted, no needed, to know if Wesley had survived Murdock.

Surely, that would be in the Wesson family history.

"I brought you dinner," Maud's voice intruded on his ruminations.

He welcomed the distraction. Reading about the past was going to bring home the fact that everything and everyone he had ever known was dead, gone forever.

He had jumped so far in the future that eleven generations of his family had lived and died. It was a sobering thought.

"You look sad," Maud observed.

Winter sighed. "Maud, I came here to rescue Wesley. I bragged about your century having all the information that I would ever need. And yet, here I am, none the wiser. I will have to return empty-handed."

Maud nodded. "You should look for your diaries before you leave. You would know where you hid them. Obviously, you hid them. You write about everything; you would write about your time-traveling adventure and how you met Eve."

"What about Eve?" Winter asked eagerly. He had felt an inexplicable pull to her from the very moment he had first seen her. He had been so caught up with his worry about Wesley he had not explored those feelings the way he wanted to. But now, Maud's mention of her was fanning the flames of interest.

Maud smiled. "I found this poem in the carriage house when I moved in thirty-five years ago. It was on the writing desk. It said 'Winter's Eve,' dated March 1721. I was dying to tell you about it."

"What did it say?" Winter asked.

"I assumed you wrote it. It was signed- Love Winter. You write 'f' for 's' in all your documents. I made a copy of it. Here it is."

Winter took the paper from her; he didn't know what she was talking about until he saw the long 's'.

"It's not 'f,' it's a long 's' or medial 's.' Our customs are so dissimilar, it's as if we don't exist in the same place."

Maud chuckled. "You can read the poem later. I made you jerk chicken and rice and peas with vegetables. Everything except the rice is grown on this farm."

"It smells perfect, Maud."

Maud nodded. "I'll be back later with the modern clothes that Willie bought for you last year. I had them washed and stored at my place. Miss Eve is right; you can't wear your old clothes around the place. She won't take you seriously in them. You will also need a haircut; I will arrange for a barber to come and attend to you. Do you remember how to use the shower?"

"I do," Winter nodded. "It was a pleasant, quick experience, and with hot water, too."

"We do it every day," Maud reminded him.

Winter laughed. "That is one thing my foreign mother did that had the servants' tongues wagging, and she insisted that we do it too. My brother Walker is especially a stickler for taking frequent swims in the stream a mile from here. Is it still here in this century?"

"It is," Maud nodded. "I'm sorry, no insult intended. I am well-versed in your time period, and I know that the custom of the upper classes was to bathe as seldom as possible."

Winter nodded. "You are not wrong."

"There must have been quite a stench in your time," Maud

shook her head. "I could not bear it. I love a good-smelling man. I keep the bathroom stocked with shower gels, rags, and cologne. Sir Bradley used to exclusively use a brand called Savage; I swear one sniff of that was all it took for me to get excited. I left a bottle for you on the armoire."

Winter chuckled. "I assume Sir Bradley is my descendant whom you had a child with."

"That's the one," Maud nodded. "You have a good memory. I told you that last year."

"Yes, Maud. As I recall, we had this same conversation; you said I smelled like a horse at the time."

Maud laughed. "You did have a horsey odor."

"I will endeavor to smell more like a savage," Winter grinned. "Maybe Eve will have the same sentiments about me as you had with Sir Bradley."

"You are such a quick learner," Maud smiled. "I like you, Winter. From the moment I came to work here when I was twenty, I looked at your portrait, and I liked you. I never thought of you as a dead person, if that makes sense."

"It makes sense to me," Winter said.

"I will return with your clothes," Maud said.

When Maud left, he read the poem. It was his writing; he could identify it anywhere.

"You are mine, and I am yours,
You are Winter's Eve,
I would defy the hands of time and, in your love, believe.
For in your eyes, I see my home,
A haven pure and true,
With every breath, I'm drawn to you,
My love, forever new.
So let the seasons come and go,
In your arms, I'll find reprieve,

For you are mine, and I am yours,
Together, we'll never leave."

She was going to mean something to him, Winter sighed. He had sensed this from the moment he first saw her.

And now this. Reading his words of love for her felt strange, but his emotions were getting there; it was not hard to imagine him saying, 'for in your eyes I see my home'.

Chapter Five

"**H**ow was your gala last night?" Winter stood in the doorway, and Eve jumped; she had not heard him come into the office. She had a bell installed at the outer office to alert her when she had visitors, but it seemed as if it was not working.

"It was okay," Eve said. "I didn't stay till the end. I went home and was out like a light as soon as my head hit the pillow. How was your night? I see you have changed into modern clothing."

"It takes a little bit of getting used to," he looked down at himself, "pants to your ankles and shirts with perfectly round buttons. How do they get them so round, do you know?"

"I have no clue," Eve said. "I expect they have machines that make them at a certain size. I never consider how these things work; I just wear them."

Winter chuckled. "Everything in this world is cause for

wonder. In my time, things are just coming into play. Just this year, Lady Mary Wortley Montagu introduced the practice of smallpox inoculation to Britain. Unfortunately, we currently have a smallpox outbreak. I heard it's all but nonexistent this time."

Eve sighed, "Can you be normal for one minute and be honest with me? Where are you from? Why are you here?"

"I will have to prove it to you," Winter said. "You will not believe a mere telling. I expect you already know a potted version of my history. I was born to an English father and a mixed-race mother; she was native Brazilian and Portuguese.

"My father met my mother in Brazil while he was searching for gold. He found plenty, much more than he had ever hoped for. He built his home in Brazil and expected to live there with his wife. Instead, he was summoned to England when his brother died from the dreaded smallpox; he became the Duke of Wesson.

"My father took my mother with him because he wasn't going to live without her. She was not accepted in society; she was too foreign, she didn't speak English very well, and she was too exotic-looking. That made her very unhappy; she hated England, but she loved my father. She endured the weather, the prejudices, and racism and bore my father four sons: Willhelm, Winter, Walker, and Wesley. I am Winter."

Eve grimaced. "Okay, I give up. You don't want to tell me your true origins. However, I am fascinated by Winter Wesson's story, so go on."

Winter smiled. "When my father became the Duke of Wesson, he inherited all the ducal lands that his father had. He also had his Brazilian interests. I grew up with the finest of things, but I also had a taste for adventure. I was inclined to explore. I read 'The Travels of Marco Polo,' an account of Marco Polo's travels as a Venetian merchant across Asia and the Far East.

"The Decameron is a collection of novellas featuring stories of adventure, romance, and wit told by ten young people who fled Florence to escape the Black Death. Some of the tales involve journeys, quests, and encounters with fantastical elements.

"And 'The Discoveries of the World' by Antonio Pigafetta. That was required reading at Eton.

"Pigafetta was an Italian scholar and explorer who accompanied Ferdinand Magellan on the first circumnavigation of the globe. His writings provide a detailed firsthand account of the voyage, including encounters with indigenous peoples and various adventures at sea.

"I wanted to do my own version of those books, and because I am the second son, my father gave me his blessing, and off I went. The first time I traveled, I did so alone with my crew. I recorded everything, collected artifacts, listened to stories, and immersed myself in the cultures of the world. I loved it."

Eve was staring at him transfixed.

Winter continued, "It was in Jerusalem where I found a merchant who was selling the sundial. He was a little man who talked too fast and looked shifty, but I bought the sundial off him."

"What language did they speak in Jerusalem in 1720?" Eve inquired.

Winter smiled, "The year was 1708, and the languages spoken were Hebrew, Arabic, and Ladino."

"Ladino?" Eve raised her eyebrows.

"Judeo-Spanish. Quite close to this century's Spanish," Winter explained.

"Oh," Eve cleared her throat.

"The man I bought the sundial from spoke Hebrew. I am fluent in Hebrew."

"I see," Eve murmured.

Winter chuckled, "And Ladino, too. In some respects, Spanish and Portuguese had similarities, at least in my time. It was not hard for me to learn either language. I grew up multilingual; my mother spoke to us in Portuguese, and my father encouraged it because we had business interests in Brazil."

"Let me test that," Eve said as she opened her laptop. "I'm going to play something in Portuguese, and you'll tell me what the person is saying."

Winter nodded in wonder. "Your devices can do anything."

She played a long paragraph from her language app, and Winter easily translated it.

"Oh my, you really can speak Portuguese," Eve looked at him. "Let me try you with Hebrew."

He easily did the same.

"It's reassuring to know that the old languages have not undergone many changes like English has," he said. "Just last night, I had to tell Maud that a long 's' was not an 'f'. This century does not use the medial 's' anymore."

Eve closed the laptop and leaned back in her chair. "It doesn't prove anything. But tell me more about Winter Wesson's story. How old were you? I mean, was he there when you/he bought the sundial?"

"Twenty," Winter said. "I sailed the Middle East, stayed on the shores of Egypt, went to various countries, fought pirates, heard stories, and immersed myself in various cultures. I was twenty-two when I made it to the Jamaican shores.

"I looked up and saw the hills in the late evening sun, and I bought the hill for myself and got the craftsmen and indentured servants to build the house. It took them three years to clear the land and build the house.

"In the meantime, I went to England to visit my father. I got word that my mother was ailing so I needed to see her, too. While there, I was coerced into marrying Beatrix Whithorn, the only surviving child of the Duke of Whithorn; he needed heirs for his ducal lands. The arrangement was that my first son would be his."

"So you did a business marriage?" Eve asked.

"Most marriages in my century and in my social class are business marriages," Winter said. "There are hardly any romantic matches, though I am sure there are some. I have never heard of them."

"So, did you grow to love her?" Eve asked, a hint of jealousy in her tone. She didn't know why she was jealous. This man was not Winter Wesson. He told a good story, though, and he had her at the edge of her seat, waiting for more.

"I did not," Winter said. "I chafed under married life to Beatrix; alas, she didn't have much of a personality. She was a devout Puritan, and she believed that every aspect of life should be governed by strict religious principles. It made for a rather dull existence, I must admit.

"Our interactions were limited to societal obligations and the occasional polite conversation. There was no genuine connection between us, no shared interests or passions. It was a marriage of convenience, nothing more." Winter paused, a wistful expression crossing his face. "She bore me two sons; the first child, Sebastien, was to become the Duke of Whithorn. His grandfather took him under his wings. The second child, Arthur, was to inherit all I had. He was my heir."

Eve opened her laptop and searched for Lady Beatrix

Wesson. She found an oil painting.

"She looks pale," Eve murmured.

"Let me see," Winter leaned forward.

Eve spun her computer around, and he nodded. "That's Beatrix, plump and pale. The portrait is quite accurate."

Eve chuckled. "I guess that was what men found attractive then."

"I did not," Winter said. "I have always gravitated to women of a darker hue."

Eve smiled. "So what happened to Beatrix?"

"She died from influenza."

"The flu?" Eve shook her head. "These days, nobody dies from the flu."

"I know," Winter said. "I found that out the second time I came here. I was concerned about the diseases in this century."

"You know a lot about Winter Wesson, his family, and his life. We could really use you in the great house tours. You would kill it."

"Kill it?" Winter raised his eyebrows.

"A modern expression," Eve said. "You'd be good at it. You would give the story an authentic edge. I can see you standing under his portrait, looking exactly like him and speaking in the first person."

"I wish I could help you," Winter said, "but I am only here to find information on the pirate Murdock; he kidnapped my brother, Wesley. Your Internet does not help, and I cannot find my writings from 1719 or 1720. I think they are around here somewhere."

"Mmm," Eve said, "where could Winter Wesson's writings be?"

"You're not taking me seriously, Eve. I need to find out where Murdock's lair is and retrieve my brother. He is terrified right now. Well, back in 1720. I guess from your perspective, he is long dead; his children's children are long dead."

Eve sighed. He was so handsome, especially now with his dark green eyes. It was an unusual color; she had never seen anybody with his shade of eyes. Well, except for the portrait in the ballroom of this very building. She had thought the artist had done some embellishment, but his eyes really were the shade of polished marble.

He could take on a role as Superman; he had a Henry Cavil look to him, with his strong jawline and chiseled features. She was a sucker for chiseled features, whatever the complexion of the male. And it didn't help that he had a banging body too, in his tight black polo t-shirt, his biceps rippling under the fabric, only added to his allure.

But it wasn't just his looks that drew her in; it was the way he carried himself, with a quiet confidence that seemed to command attention without him even trying. And yet, despite his striking appearance and undeniable charisma, there was a vulnerability in his eyes, a look that hinted at hidden depths and secrets yet to be uncovered.

Eve felt her heart rate increase. Did someone suddenly turn off the AC? She felt hot under the collar, just staring at him. He returned the look, his smile growing wider and wider as their eyes held.

"If you help me find my diaries, I am sure you will be mentioned in there," Winter said softly. "That will be your proof."

Eve dragged her eyes from his. "Me?"

"I have written about you; there's a poem entitled Winter's Eve. I am sure there are other writings. I feel more attracted to you than I have felt with any other."

He admitted his attraction to her so easily. Eve inhaled;

she couldn't deny the pull she felt towards him as well, but she wasn't ready to admit to it just yet. She was tempted to ask what the poem, Winter's Eve, said but held back. Maybe Winter, knew someone named Eve. If that were the case, it would make for a huge coincidence. She didn't want to be indulging in fantasies. Romantic fantasy was what got her into a two-year marriage with David.

She changed the subject, trying to mask her own emotions.

"Well, if you're so sure that Winter had those diaries, you should try to find them," Eve said, steering the conversation back to the topic at hand.

"But where on earth would I have put them in this place?" Winter said. "I can understand putting them in a library; that's where all my papers and books were placed. Why make a treasure hunt for my diaries, especially for those crucial years?"

"That's an intriguing question," Eve said. "Why would Winter Wesson hide those diaries? Maybe because he doesn't want imposters rifling through his secrets."

Winter laughed. "I had no secrets."

"Maybe you heard the speculation of some historians that a whole shipment of gold is buried somewhere on this property. And you think Winter has the treasure map in one of his later diaries. Is that why you are here?"

Winter shook his head. "I just want the diaries. I will leave the treasure hunting to you."

"You know what?" Eve said, "I will help you look for the diaries. Just to ensure that you are not removing valuable information from the Crimson Hill Great House. Those diaries are our property."

"Is that the only reason?" Winter raised an eyebrow, "Are you sure you don't believe me even a little?"

"Quite sure," Eve said, "For now, I am merely intrigued."

Chapter Six

Eve decided to help Fake Winter search for the diaries the next day because she wanted to confirm that he was an impostor, but the minute he strolled into the carriage house, he started pointing out hiding places. Her skepticism was horribly battered. Maud and Willie willingly helped to upend their living room area, eagerly anticipating what he would find in the nooks and crannies of the place.

They didn't find anything of note except for a pouch of silver coins under the floorboards where Maud's center table sat atop a carpet. He had them remove the carpet and lift up two loose floorboards.

"Those are silver ducats," Winter said when Willie took out the pouch and spread the coins on the table. "Someone took out the gold ones."

"That's really money from the eighteenth century? It's in mint condition." Eve opened her eyes wide while she held up the silver coins to the light. My goodness, how did you know about this? And why do you call them ducats?"

"This was an actual carriage house. We sometimes keep money under the floorboards for emergencies. Ducats are a type of currency from my time. They were widely used for trade and were made of silver or gold, depending on their value," Winter said, disappointment rife in his voice.

Eve reached for her phone, "How much would ten pieces of silver ducat be worth in this time? I think we can display these, but we must know what we are doing; I don't want people to rob us." Eve quickly tapped away on her phone, searching for current market prices of antique coins. After a moment, she looked up, her eyes widening. "According to what I found, ten pieces of silver ducats from the eighteenth century could be worth thousands of dollars, potentially even tens of thousands, depending on their rarity and condition!"

"I told you he was the real Winter Wesson," Maud cackled. "I saw him appearing beside the sundial with my own two eyes."

Her skepticism was slowly fading. Eve cleared her throat. "Well, Winter, what's next?"

Winter found it amusing. "I am much heartened, Eve, that thou hast dropped the 'Fake' from my name."

"I am still not convinced. Maybe your name is Winter. Maybe your parents saw how similar you looked to the original Winter and named you accordingly."

Winter laughed.

"I am heading home," Eve said, giving Willie the pouch. "Put it back where you found it. We'll pick this up tomorrow."

"Where is home?" Winter asked as they walked toward the parking lot.

"An apartment in town," Eve said. "I couldn't face living in my marital home anymore. Too many memories of how stupid I was."

"Your previous husband was the stupid one," Winter said.

"Are you flattering me for something," Eve asked, "or is your interest in me genuine?"

"Genuine," Winter said, "I have quite unexpectedly taken a liking to you. I wish you didn't have to go and that we could spend some time together."

"I have quite unexpectedly taken a shine to you too," Eve said, "and for that, I am questioning my sanity because, after David, I have vowed that in my next relationship, I want no games, just pure honesty, but so far you seem to be acting.

"I am not the kind of girl you play around with. When I love, I love hard. I play for keeps. My favorite quality in a man is honesty."

"I see finding the coins was not convincing," Winter nodded. "Well, tomorrow we try again, Eve. I think honesty is my favorite quality in a woman too."

He stood back, and she got in the car. She watched him in the rearview mirror until it was impossible to see him anymore. There was a flutter of anticipation for what tomorrow might bring.

Despite her reservations, a part of her yearned to explore this unexpected attraction to Winter, or whoever he was.

****

The next day, she found a note under her office door. It was a poem.

When I could not sleep last night,
Thoughts of you kept me alight.
In dreams, your laughter filled the air,
Your smile is a light beyond compare.

In your presence, I find my calm,
A soothing balm, a healing psalm.
Though words may falter, my feelings are true,
Know that my heart beats just for you.
So let us seize this day anew,
And see where our journey takes us, me and you.

Yours always,
Winter

He was poetic, she mused. She was anticipating seeing him, too. He showed up a little after nine o'clock.

"Good morning, Eve."

"Good morning, Winter. Thank you for the lovely poem."

Winter smiled. "I like putting my thoughts into words. It's an honest expression of mine."

Eve chuckled. "Okay."

"I came to ask permission to search the main house this evening. Maud said I should ask you before I proceed because you are fastidious about the tour schedule and having me underfoot in the main house could cause a stampede."

"She is right," Eve nodded. "Your presence could be distracting. Unless... you want to put on the old costume, greet the last group, give them a tour, and see how it goes."

"No, thank you," Winter said. "Showing a bunch of strangers my home and speaking of myself in the past tense is not desirable to me at this time."

"So what are you going to do today?" Eve asked.

"I will stay in this office with you, over at that desk browsing the computer. I am particularly interested in the inner workings of the vehicle I saw you driving yesterday."

Eve nodded. "Okay, as long as you do not distract me."

"I will be as quiet as a mouse," Winter assured her as he sat down at Rosalita's desk. "How do you turn this one on? It is quite different from Craig's machine."

Eve sighed. "This is called a desktop; Craig's is a laptop."

"Ah," Winter nodded.

Eve observed his serious expression. Surely no modern person could keep up the act for this long without slipping. She turned on the computer and showed him the relevant buttons, and pretty soon, he was happily engaged with the inner workings of cars. He was as attentive as if he were watching an action-packed movie.

"Use your headphones for the videos," she instructed, giving him a new pair and showing him how to use them.

He really was the perfect companion for the day.

Chapter Seven

"**T**he things I saw today on the internet," Winter said to her after she closed up the office. "I had no idea they were possible; I need a few years to process all of the information I just consumed."

Eve chuckled; he looked genuinely in awe. "What did you learn today?"

"I found out about combustion engines and how they power vehicles, how electricity can be harnessed to illuminate cities, and how information can be transmitted across vast distances through telecommunication networks. It's all quite remarkable, isn't it?" Winter's eyes gleamed with newfound understanding and curiosity.

Eve nodded. "I have always taken humanities advancements for granted. I have never thought how incredible it would be for somebody from the eighteenth century. You jumped quite a couple of steps to be here. From carriages drawn by horses to cars operated by electricity."

"I haven't touched on that yet," Winter said. "Tomorrow, I want to learn about electricity. I want to know how the touch of a switch can give you instant light."

Eve nodded. "Sounds fun."

"Is there instant light in the great house?" Winter asked.

"Yes," Eve nodded. "It was wired for electricity in the early twentieth century."

They scoured the fourteen-room main house slowly, with Winter pointing to potential hiding areas. If Eve was not quite a believer, she was becoming one as Winter confidently found hidden areas around the house that she didn't know exist.

Their final stop was the main bedroom with its canopied king-sized bed and sheets that resembled their three-hundred-year counterparts.

Winter stood in the middle of the room and spun around. "I had a desk right there. It's no longer there. I would sit and write by candlelight way into the night."

"What did you write with?" Eve asked.

Winter paused, a nostalgic glint in his dark green eyes. "Quill and ink." His voice tinged with a hint of wistfulness. "I had a favorite quill, a gift from my father. It had a smooth, delicate nib that glided across the parchment like a dancer on a stage." He smiled faintly, lost in the memories of nights spent immersed in his writing. "The ink was a deep, rich black, and the flickering flame of the lamp cast shadows that danced along the edges of my thoughts as I put pen to paper." He turned to Eve, his expression earnest. "Those were the moments when I felt most alive, when the words flowed freely from my mind, weaving tales of adventure, love, and discovery. I enjoyed writing almost as much as the adventures themselves."

Eve sat on the bed. Her skepticism was slowly melting

away. This man was too passionate about finding the diaries for this to be a hoax. He had not slipped once, his accent, the inflections on his words, the obvious frustrations of not finding the diaries. His genuine reactions to anything new.

"Say I believe that you somehow time traveled," Eve said, "how did it happen?"

"I thought you would never ask," Winter said, standing at the window and looking out at the waning sun. The main bedroom faced the front lawn, where the sundial was. Beyond the gates, it was blurry, as if the place was not in focus.

"Tell me, what do you see beyond the gates?" he asked Eve.

Eve got up and stood beside him. "I see trees, many trees."

"Sharp and in focus?" Winter asked.

"Well, yes," Eve nodded.

"I can't see them in focus," Winter said. "For me, beyond the gates resides my timeline. I think the sundial is a time portal; it connects our two timelines. I am trying to figure out how or why. The middle dial of the sundial turns, and I can only line it up with this timeline. I've tried to adjust it to others, but my time and yours seem to run concurrently. A two-day lapse in this time is a two-day lapse in my time.

"Our dates are different, though, because we use different calendars. September in my time may be July in yours. I have been here twice before, and both times have coincided with an equinox. That's when the day and night are of equal length."

Eve nodded. "So, if I understand correctly, the sundial acts as a bridge between our two time periods, allowing you to travel back and forth between them?"

"Exactly," he confirmed. "But there's still much I don't understand about how it works or why it brought me here."

Eve glanced at the mysterious sundial, its ancient stone surface weathered by time yet holding the key to untold secrets.

"Are you the only one who can travel between times?"

"It seems so," Winter said. "My brother tried it but to no avail. Even my manservant Cornelius has tried it but nothing happens. When I get to this time, I cannot leave the boundaries of the great house. If I walk through the gates now, I will be in my timeline. The last time I left here, I was in modern clothes; I ended up naked in my timeline."

Eve snickered.

"I can only visit this time twice a year when there is an equinox, but I can go back to my time whenever I please; all I need to do is walk through the gates. I wish you could come with me and see what the past looked like—just once."

"No," Eve was horrified. "Winter, if what you are saying is even remotely true, you live in a time of slavery and gender inequality. I don't want to visit an era where I am considered the weaker sex because I am a woman and, worse, less than an animal because I am black.

"No, thank you. The seventeenth century was not good for my people or my gender. Neither were the eighteenth, nineteenth, or twentieth, but the seventeenth century would be horrible for a black woman. I read somewhere that the life expectancy of a slave was five years after capture, and that was considered long. I like this timeline, thank you very much. At least in my time and in this part of the world, I have a voice."

"It's interesting hearing you describe the eighteenth century so starkly. I imagine we do seem a little backward."

"A little?" Eve chuckled. "And I haven't even touched on the fashions of the day. What were those big hoop things that the women used to wear? And don't let me get started on the hygiene."

"And to imagine, I thought my era was quite enlightened."

Eve laughed. "Oh no."

"So if we were to be together I would have to stay here, in your time?"

"Definitely," Eve nodded. "It is a far better century for us to be as an interracial couple."

Winter nodded. "There is that."

"Not that I am suggesting we should be a couple," Eve hurriedly added.

"Why not?" Winter asked. "Since you've entered my life, everything has felt different—more vibrant, more alive. You challenge me, you inspire me, and in your presence I feel like I've discovered a piece of myself that I never knew was missing."

Eve's heart fluttered at his words, her mind grappling with the whirlwind of emotions swirling inside her. "We just met."

"And yet you recognized me," Winter touched her hand, "just like I recognized you, maybe you drew me here."

His touch sending a shiver down her spine. "Admit it, Eve."

"I felt a certain awareness," Eve nodded. "But I…" she gazed into his dark green eyes, feeling a sense of déjà vu.

She shook away the feeling. "I am going home. I'll see you tomorrow."

Winter nodded and watched her as she walked away.

Chapter Eight

Eve couldn't sleep that night. She had gone to bed super early; it was probably not even nine o'clock. Her apartment building was unusually noisy, or was this how it was at this time of night? She usually watched television, allowing whatever was on to drown out the outside noise.

But tonight, she didn't feel like watching anything. The words "maybe you drew me here" kept repeating in her head. There were echoes of truth in there somewhere. She did not have to work at Crimson Hills Great House. The offer to work there had just fallen into her lap; it seemed out of nowhere. She was an accountant, and she hated working for the company she was at. She bellyached about the job while her father listened.

"So why don't you come and work with me?" he had asked.

"And if I hate working with you, who will I complain to?" Eve had joked. "You are my shoulder to cry on, my listening ear. Besides, you already have an accountant."

Her father nodded, "You have a point, but you don't have to do accounts. Have you considered property management?"

"I haven't," Eve said, "but I am intrigued."

"Good, I got a call from the head of the Wesson Board of Trustees, Stuart Smithson," her father explained. "He said they are sending out feelers for a property manager for one of their properties, Crimson Hill Great House. He doesn't want my company to manage it; they would prefer someone working for them exclusively, and he somehow asked for you by name."

"I'll do it," Eve said.

"You hate your job at Greggor and Sanchez that bad?" Her father had asked incredulously.

"No, not really…I like the sound of Crimson Hills. What does the job entail?"

"It's a great house, nearly three hundred years old," her father explained. "They have tours of the place; they run a gift shop. The property manager's post would be quite varied. You'd be overseeing the maintenance of the historic property, ensuring it meets safety and preservation standards for visitors, managing staff for the tours and gift shop, coordinating events and special occasions held at the house, and handling any administrative tasks related to its operation. It's a unique opportunity to immerse yourself in history and hospitality while utilizing your organizational and managerial skills."

"I want it!" Eve had said excitedly.

And now here she was, property manager of Winter Wessons' house, more than half convinced that he had indeed traveled through time.

She flung the sheets off her legs. She had been offered a place to stay; she could have lived on the property if she had desired, but she was married then and didn't mind the commute.

It would have been more convenient for her to stay there now. Why had she rented this apartment anyway? It was a waste of money. She only came by to sleep. She usually grabbed dinner from the Silver Spoon restaurant on her way home and breakfast when she was going to the great house. She spent weekends in her old room at her parents' house.

She could just as easily pack her things in her parents' pool house and only take what was necessary to Crimson Hills and stay there. It would save her a ton of money on gas. She would be doing something for the environment, and she would be closer to Winter.

Though she had not admitted it to him, she recognized him on some level. She needed to find out why he was there and what was driving her towards him.

****

Eve moved into the counter's cottage for the next two days. Winter and Willie helped her as she carted a few suitcases and boxes into the cottage. She had a mini fridge, a hot plate, a microwave, and a cupboard to put her snacks. That's all she needed, really. She would make her own breakfast and have her food delivered from Silver Spoon.

"You don't need to do that, Miss Eve!" Maud protested when she heard her plans. "I can make breakfast and dinner for you. It's not a problem and at no additional expense. I get most of my ingredients from the farm anyway. You love my cooking, don't you?"

Eve nodded. She loved Maud's cooking but did not want to impose on her.

"Take advantage of the bounties of the farm," Maud said,

"just tell me what you like."

And so she was sorted.

On her first night as a resident, Winter came by, and they chatted into the wee hours of the morning. They sat on the veranda, and he told her tales of his adventures at sea.

"I traveled the world," he said. "I went up the Atlantic Ocean to as far as Siberia and then back to the Pacific. Then, I made several stops in the Indian Ocean. We spent months in Bombay. East India is a British stronghold."

"Was," Eve chuckled.

"Do we still own any country?" Winter asked in despair.

Eve shook her head. "Not in the traditional sense, no. The era of colonialism has largely ended, with countries gaining independence from their former colonizers."

Winter sighed, gazing out into the night sky. "I suppose that's for the best. It's just strange to think about how much has changed in the world since the 1700s. It seemed so important to us to conquer and rule then. We used to have so many skirmishes with the Dutch, French, Spanish, and Portuguese. It was a race to conquer the various lands, and the natives were collateral damage."

"The world keeps evolving," Eve said. "In this post-colonial era, we are learning to value cooperation, respect, and diversity rather than seeking domination. We strive for understanding and collaboration among nations. The transition has its challenges. Jamaica, for instance, has not totally moved away from her colonial past. We still have the reigning British monarch as our head of state. But despite these lingering connections, we have forged our own identity, embraced our culture, and asserted our independence on the global stage. Jamaica's population is majority black now."

Winter nodded thoughtfully. "I will tell my manservant, Cornelius, this news when I go back."

"Your manservant is black?" Eve asked.

"Yes," Winter nodded. "He joined us while we were docked at St. Helena several years ago. He was sold into slavery by his own people to a couple called the Raffertys. They were very nice to him, but Cornelius is too proud to be a slave and too intelligent to be subservient. He found us when we were about to leave St. Helena and offered to work for us for pay. His exact words to me were, 'I find the concept of slavery to be too low-brow for my tastes. I will do an honest day's work for an honest day's pay and be a loyal servant for you in return.'

"We accepted his terms, and he has been with my brother Walker and me ever since. We debate a lot; he and I. Walker is usually our referee when our arguments become too heated."

"Rafferty!" Eve widened her eyes. "Oh, my word. Does he call himself Cornelius Rafferty?"

"Yes," Winter nodded.

"We just bought back Rafferty House from the heirs. It is two miles from here and was built a few years after the great house. We have records saying it was leased to the Rafferty family for a couple of hundred years until it was sold to them outright after the Wesson family started selling pockets of the land in the early twentieth century, as outlined by the trustee agreement. We bought back Rafferty House just recently. I don't think the board of trustees quite knows what to do with it yet."

"I would live there. It is such a nice place. It's close to work, and I wouldn't constantly be living in a show house, but the board refused to sell it. They snatched it up as soon as it became available."

Winter looked at her contemplatively. "What year did it become available?"

"Earlier this year," Eve shook her head. "Anyway, I don't think it is a coincidence that it is called Rafferty House; it has been in the Rafferty family for generations."

Winter smiled. "Cornelius is our brother in arms. Walker and I would have made sure his future was secure."

"Winter and Walker," Eve chuckled, "let me guess, you were born in winter, and he walked out of the womb."

Winter laughed. "You are mostly right. I was born in winter; my mother saw Walker's sturdy, chubby legs and said he will be a walker."

Eve chuckled.

"That's how my mother's tribe named their offspring. My father allowed it for us; however, my older brother was named Willhelm because he was the first and would be a duke, and it is a traditional Wesson name. My youngest brother, Wesley, is so named because he was born in the house's west wing." Winter grinned. "My mother would have called him West but compromised with my dad, who said Wesley sounded more polished."

Eve chuckled. "A creative naming tradition your family has."

Winter nodded. "Indeed, it adds a bit of character to our family tree. So what about your family? Tell me about you."

"My parents are Veronica and Thaddeus Blair. They met at a church function when they were sixteen. They both said it was love at first sight."

"I like that term," Winter said. "I think I understand what it means."

Eve looked at him and then cleared her throat. "I don't believe in it. I mean, I used to, but not anymore. My parents are the exception. They truly jibe. They mesh well. They are a unique, successful love story."

"My mother is an overachiever, a top lawyer; she has her

own law firm. My dad is a realtor; he has his own business. They had me and my sister, Evita."

"Evita," Winter murmured. "I like the name."

"Me too," Eve smiled. "I was supposed to be Evelyn, but my mother used the 'Lyn' as my middle name instead."

"Where is Evita?" Winter asked.

"She is in France with her husband, Ian. They made a vow to follow each other everywhere when they were children. He got a job in France, so she followed. And there goes another successful relationship. I wanted that," Eve said wistfully. "I guess I projected all the hopes of a fairytale romance onto David. He must have seen me coming a mile away and decided to take advantage of my gullibility."

"I hate that he hurt you," Winter whispered. "Did you love him?"

"I thought so," Eve said. "Lately, I am beginning to assess myself. I am not sure I loved him. I loved the thought of him, what I wanted him to be. I loved his family. They are a great family. Looking back now, his family had much more appeal than he did."

"Where is all of this honesty coming from? It's as if the scales are gone from my eyes. David was more honest than I was. He said he didn't love me."

"Because you were not his to love," Winter said, curling his hand around hers. "Our fates are tied together, Eve Blair."

Eve gazed at him, she was beginning to believe that. She had no words to describe it, but she was beginning to feel a deep resonance between herself and Winter as if they were two halves of a whole destined to find each other.

It was a connection beyond mere words or rational explanation. It was something primal and undeniable coursing through her veins. In his presence, she felt understood in a way she never had before, as though he held the missing pieces of her soul.

The warmth of Winter's touch comforted her. Eve realized that perhaps her past struggles and heartaches had led her to this moment — to him. Despite the pain of her past, she found solace in the possibility of a future where she could be truly seen and loved for who she was.

She squeezed his fingers. "I am going to agree with you."

"Tell me about the board of trustees and how they operate," Winter said.

"The board of trustees is entrusted with the responsibility of overseeing assets such as property, investments, or funds. They ensure they're managed according to the wishes outlined in the trust agreement."

"A trust agreement?" Winter raised his eyebrows.

"Yes, a trust agreement," Eve continued. "Trustees must act in the best interests of the beneficiaries, following specific guidelines set out in the trust document or by law. This includes making investment decisions, distributing income or assets, and handling any administrative tasks related to the trust."

"I like that," Winter said.

"Tell me something," Eve asked, "is this your first time hearing about a board of trustees?"

"Yes, I have been curious to know how it works," Winter said.

"So that means I started it?" Eve frowned. "If we didn't have this conversation, would there be a board of trustees for the Wesson properties? Time travel is a conundrum."

"I know about trusts," Winter said, "but I never thought of using one. I assumed Arthur would inherit my properties and then his children, and so on and so on. But with a trust, I can ensure that the assets are managed and distributed according to my wishes even after I'm gone.

"It offers a level of control and protection that a simple inheritance plan might not provide. Plus, it allows for flexibility in how assets are utilized for the benefit of future generations rather than relying solely on the decisions of individual heirs. It's definitely an intriguing concept. I guess, in a way, you are responsible for me thinking about it."

Eve nodded. "I feel powerful. I just created the Wesson Board of Trustees. I hope I get an honorary mention in your trust agreement. Now, that would be wild."

It would be, Winter said thoughtfully.

Chapter Nine

Winter tossed and turned in bed after talking to Eve. Now that he was alone, his mind was on his mission. The reason why he had crossed centuries in the first place, was in a desperate bid to find where Wesley was taken by Murdock and to do something about it.

Today would be four days since they had gotten the ransom note from Murdock's intermediary.

Deliver a shipment of gold, or we will use his head as a drinking cup.

The gruesome message had been chilling.

"Didn't you say that you can learn anything in the twenty-first century?" Walker asked him as they paced the library together.

"My people call it the sky records," Cornelius said, "where the holy man can access the entire history of every soul of creation since the dawn of creation. Not just our creation but the creation of other worlds. You can view their thoughts and feelings and the words they uttered at any given moment in time from the moment they are born to the time they go back to Source. It is a powerful tool, indeed."

"No," Winter said, "it's not a sky record. You are speaking of otherworldly things. This is very much of this world, a scientific invention created in their time by them, if memory serves me correctly, in the late twentieth century. It is a collection of information about all the earthly happenings, even from our time. They call it an interconnected network or Internet."

"Can we trust it?" Walker asked. "This information source, and would they know about Wesley?"

"I think so," Winter nodded. "They have technology you would not believe, moving pictures with accurate depictions of places. It's real as if you've been there yourself. They even have portraits of men before our time and their stories. They have vehicles that fly, so you can travel from here to England in a day."

"Tell me more," Cornelius said.

"He has gone over that for months and months," Walker said frustratedly, "you should write it somewhere, Cornelius, so that you can read it for yourself. For now, we must focus on Wesley."

Winter nodded, "I will go to their time, retrieve the information, and get back here with it. We are about to have a vernal equinox. I should prepare."

"I wish I could time travel," Cornelius said wistfully.

"You would love it," Winter said, "our countrymen used your countrymen to build the island; eventually, we were outnumbered. Maud said your people were emancipated from slavery in 1838."

Cornelius frowned. "That's one hundred and sixty-three years from now!"

Winter looked at his friend. The news obviously distressed him.

"Don't be distressed, Cornelius. Britain officially abolished slavery at that time. The Maroons were never enslaved; they are fighting back. Even in our time, there are uprisings and revolts every day, it seems."

"We never won a war in the interior of this island; I think that is why so many slaves were brought here in the first place. There was a constant need for labor because the people kept running away. A mere nineteen years from now, the government will reach an agreement with them and allow them their freedom."

"Good," Cornelius nodded. "I admire the Maroons."

"This country will have two governments," Winter said, "the formal and the informal one."

"That's what your people get for slavery," Cornelius smirked.

"The Portuguese started the slave trade, and the British will end it," Winter said. "According to the records, we were the ones who put an end to slavery."

"After you participated," Cornelius pointed out. "Besides, aren't you a quarter Portuguese? So, in effect, a quarter of your heritage is responsible for starting slavery."

"And half of my heritage put an end to it," Winter rebutted. "And please don't forget it was your own people who sold you to the Portuguese as a slave. Which, by your logic, would mean a hundred percent of your heritage participated in slavery. Let's not forget that Africans sell Africans. Europeans would not be so successful with the slave trade if they did not have the eager help of Africans. If you want to point a finger, Cornelius, I suggest you look at your own people."

Cornelius grimaced. "You have a point. The slave trade

would not have been successful if we did not participate. There is enough blame to go around. Can we move on?"

Walker chuckled. "He always gets you with that little fact, doesn't he?"

"Yes," Cornelius grumbled.

"Back to the topic at hand, freeing Wesley, who will surely be dead if we don't do something."

And that's when they had planned what he should do. He should find out where Murdock was, and then they would ambush him and finish his obsession with them. They had long theorized that Murdock was targeting their ships and family because he was a former gold prospector who thought it would be more lucrative to rob the ships transferring gold than to work for it.

But their gold shipments were heavily protected, so he had to settle for kidnapping whichever Wesson he could find and demanding a ransom.

Murdock had captured him once, and they had fought. He had underestimated Winter's fighting skills. Winter had learned the art of self-defense from Shaolin monks. He had spent six months with them learning their arts and Murdock had felt the brunt of their teachings.

Murdock had feared him, and if his men had not rescued him at the time, Winter would have finished him. He had made an enemy, and Murdock's once lazy intentions to rob them of gold now took on a tinge of malice.

And he had his brother.

He had been so sure coming to this century would help him find Murdock's lair, but he would return to his timeline empty-handed.

Winter got up. He had had enough of trying to sleep. Craig's computer was on the writing table. He opened it, willing to give searching the Internet another try. He hadn't found information on Murdock, but maybe he would find something about his own family. At least it would put his mind at rest about Wesley.

He typed in the Wesson family of Britain and the West Indies. He found a page dedicated to them on a site called Heritage and began reading.

The Wesson family stands as one of England's oldest and most esteemed lineages, tracing their noble roots back to the time of William the Conqueror. For nearly a millennium, they have been a stalwart presence in the annals of English history, their name synonymous with nobility, honor, and tradition.

The story of the Wesson family begins amidst the tumultuous years of the Norman Conquest. As William, Duke of Normandy, embarked on his historic campaign to claim the English throne, a valiant knight named Sir Geoffrey Wesson distinguished himself on the battlefield. For his unwavering loyalty and bravery, Sir Geoffrey was granted lands and titles, laying the foundation for what would become a dynasty of nobility.

Over the centuries, the Wesson family flourished, expanding their influence and prestige across the English countryside. Through shrewd diplomacy, strategic marriages, and unwavering dedication to their duties, they ascended to the ranks of ducal nobility, cementing their place as pillars of the aristocracy.

Throughout their illustrious history, the Wessons have made significant contributions to English society. From serving as trusted advisors to monarchs to leading armies in times of war, they have consistently demonstrated their unwavering commitment to the betterment of their country and its people. Whether in the halls of power or on the fields of battle, the Wessons have left an indelible mark on the tapestry of English history.

Winter stopped reading. He wanted specifics about his family, not the general rundown. He typed in Warwick Wesson, his father's name, and then he got an eyeful.

Warwick Wesson, Duke of Wesson, was born in 1660 and died in 1721. The late duke was survived by four sons: Wilhelm, Winter, Walker, and Wesley.

Winter breathed a sigh of relief. Wesley lived. And then it hit him. His father would die in 1721 from a heart attack.

His brother Willhelm was the new Duke of Wesson in 1721. He held that title for four months and then died from alcohol poisoning. His wife Anne died in childbirth shortly after.

He was next in line to the succession. He would be the next Duke of Wesson.

He scrolled the page until he found himself. They used the headshot of the portrait that he had sat for, which was now hanging in the library.

Winter Wesson was a man thought to be ahead of his time. An avid researcher and scholar, he bequeathed a gift of land to establish a free school in the parish of Trelawny for the purposes of studying science and technology. Wesson School is still in operation today.

Winter Wesson owned many properties across Jamaica. His property portfolio was extensive. In 1721, he set up a trustee board that is one of the oldest of its kind in Jamaica. The trustee agreement is still studied in schools. Unfortunately, Winter Wesson disappeared at the age of 32. A monument is erected in his honor at Crimson Hill Great House, his private residence.

Winter grimaced. Why had he disappeared?

He scrolled down the screen to Walker Wesson. They had a profile of his brother as an older man, Walker Wesson, the

Duke of Wesson, 1693-1770.

Walker had a beard and mustache. He looked a lot like their dad in the portrait. They had the same patrician features and steely blue eyes.

Winter had inherited their mother's coloring, olive-skinned, wavy black hair, and vivid green eyes. Ironically, Willhelm, the oldest, and Wesley, the youngest, fell squarely in the middle of his parent's features.

He had gotten sidetracked thinking about himself, so he scrolled back down to read more about his siblings. It felt surreal staring at his brother, who was twenty-seven back in 1720 but was now an elderly man in this photo.

Walker held the Duke title for fifty years. The duke was known for his scholarship, abolitionist stance, and emphasis on hygiene.

Winter laughed out loud. "Good for you, brother. You never changed."

He moved to Wesley Wesson, born in 1703, died in 1802, and was the author of more than thirty novels centered around pirates. His time travel novels were co-written with his wife Anastasia Seaward and a free black man named Cornelius Rafferty, which are still uncomfortably accurate. People still use Wesley Wesson's works to predict the future.

Winter stopped reading, and he didn't want to know more. Well, he did. He wanted to know how his sons feared, but knowing all of this information was making him feel saddened in a way he had never accounted for.

He should return Craig's laptop. It was of no help.

If he went missing in 1721, did that mean he was killed, kidnapped, and vanished off the face of the earth?

He would never voluntarily leave his sons. He wrote his sons every month. He should make his monthly missives twice per month.

He had the typical relationship with his children as most men did in the 1700s, distant and formal, with occasional gestures of paternal duty. He often wondered if they knew how much he cared for them despite the physical and emotional distance that separated them.

He wasn't very emotive, like his father and his father's father before him.

Winter sighed, closing the laptop and pushing it aside. They were safe in their boarding schools, as were all boys of their station. He wondered if his letters had made any impact on their lives.

The twenty-first century was doing strange things to his mind. When had he ever wondered about his letters impacting his sons?

Maybe because he was seeing things from another perspective. Had he made enough of a difference so that they could make a difference?

When he finally fell into a restless slumber, he thought about them and the adults they would become, and their children and their children.

A knock on the door woke him from his slumber. He opened it heavy-eyed.

"Rise and shine, Winter," Maud grinned. "I have breakfast for you over at the carriage house. It will fortify you for the whole day so that you can continue your search for your diaries."

Winter leaned on the doorjamb. "Maud, I am not hungry."

"You seem sad," Maud said astutely.

"I went against my vow and started reading my family history. Technically, I should know that everybody I know is long dead, but emotionally, it hits hard when seeing it in stark detail. So, I am a bit out of sorts at the moment. Besides that, I hear I went missing in 1721."

"Yes, that's our history of you," Maud nodded. "Your brother placed a monument on the front lawn and put some writings on there. It's in Latin, I memorized it a couple years ago."

"What's the Latin?" Winter asked.

"Sit iter tuum tutum et fortunatum, et experientiam tuam optimam."

"May your journey be safe and fortunate, and your experience the best." Winter smiled.

"That's it," Maud nodded. "I looked it up."

"Which brother?" Winter asked.

"Wesley," Maud said. "It must be confusing going back and forth through vastly different centuries. I know I would be confused."

"I am a relic of times past," Winter ran his hand through his hair and sat down. "A living relic."

Maud glared at him. "Snap out of it, stick to your mission. You have seen the future; make it work to your advantage. Stop with the 'woe is me' nonsense."

Winter smiled. "You sound like my mother; except she would say it in Portuguese."

Maud chuckled. "You haven't searched everywhere yet. Have you checked the kitchen? The counting house?"

Winter stood up. "No, but there is a cellar in the kitchen. I may have put it there with the whisky."

Maud smiled. "You should ask Miss Eve for the key. We only use the kitchen now when we are hosting large events, but in the meantime, you need to taste my breakfast. I went all out for you."

Chapter Ten

Eve decided to accompany Winter to the kitchen after she left work a little after five o'clock. It started to rain after they entered the space. The kitchen was large and was obviously expanded and upgraded since it was originally built, but the old fireplace was still there. He headed straight for the small fireplace. He used to keep his best whisky behind the bricked-over opening at the top. He just needed to shift a few bricks, and then he would find an open space; the question was, why would he hide documents in the kitchen? It was the place where a fire was most likely to start.

"We had the best roasted chickens in this fireplace," he murmured.

"How did that work?" Eve asked curiously.

"We put the birds on skewers and did a dozen at a time, slowly turning them so that all sides were done," Winter looked at her. "That's a custom you should not have lost. The meat was crispy outside, moist inside, and loaded with

                    BRENDA BARRETT

seasonings."

"We haven't lost it; we just upgraded it, I think," Eve said. "We do it in a rotisserie oven."

"Does your rotisserie oven give it a smoky flavor?" Winter raised his eyebrow.

"No," Eve said. "And to be honest, all the rotisserie chicken I have had to date has been a bit bland, even with seasonings added."

"So my century did something better than yours," Winter murmured as he pushed against one of the bricks, and it shifted. He began removing them one by one.

"Oh my," Eve whispered. "I am definitely surprised at this hiding place."

He grinned, enjoying seeing the astonishment on her face whenever he said or did something that proved he was from centuries gone by.

"How did you know about that?" Eve asked as he moved the bricks.

"I created it to store my whisky," Winter grunted after taking out the last stone. "And wouldn't you look at that? They are still there."

Eve was stunned; he could see it in her eyes. "But…how?"

"Do you believe me now?" Winter asked her as he took out two bottles. "The tops are still intact. It can still be had. I bought these in Port Royal at a pub called Carnage. It is still frequented by pirates and privateers. Even though the earthquake in 1692 sunk two-thirds of the town into the sea, it still has its charms, nearly thirty years later in my time."

Eve took one of the bottles and read it, "Old Style Whisky Port Royal, 70% proof."

"My goodness," she whispered.

"I wish I could see it now," Winter continued. "Does it look anything like the days of old?"

"No," Eve looked at him. "It is a sleepy fishing village, a far cry from being the Wickedest City in the world. It has experienced a couple of fires, earthquakes, and hurricanes; the shoreline is far back from where it once was. I went there on a school trip once; I couldn't envision it being a bustling city."

"Nothing lasts forever, I guess," Winter mused. "My father visited Port Royal before the earthquake in '92. He said it was a vibrant and bustling port city filled with merchants, sailors, and all manner of characters from around the world. The streets were alive with the sounds of commerce and revelry, and the air was thick with the scent of spices, rum, and sea salt. On one of my first voyages in the Atlantic Ocean, I had to stop there to see what he was talking about."

"But alas, when I visited, time and fate had taken their toll on Port Royal. It was but a shadow of its former self. I am not surprised to hear that it is now even further diminished. If this crossing of time has taught me anything, it's that there is a fleeting nature to glory and prosperity."

Eve was looking at him transfixed.

"What is it?" he asked.

"I just realized that I believe you. I believe all of this. I was beginning to believe you before, but…this is crazy. This is science fiction. I don't even like science fiction," Eve murmured. "But then, if this is real, maybe I am losing my mind."

"It is real," Winter cupped her cheek. "You're not losing your mind, Eve. Sometimes reality can be stranger than fiction, but that doesn't make it any less real."

Their eyes locked, sharing a moment of understanding that transcended words.

"We need to search the counting house; my diaries are not here. That's the last place I have to look," Winter said.

Eve nodded. "Okay, let's make a run for it. It's coming down in sheets."

Chapter Eleven

They were soaked through when they reached the counting house.

"We might as well peel off our clothes out here," Eve said. "I have an oversized robe that can fit you while I throw these in the dryer." She stripped down to her bra and panties, shivering.

Winter hadn't moved; he watched her and whispered, "As I live and breathe!"

Eve grinned. "I am sorry to shock you; I know your century is known for its modesty, but I have no intention of getting the wild orange floorboards wet if I can help it."

"I don't see any here," Winter dragged his eyes from her body.

"What?" Eve asked, completely uninhibited around him.

He swallowed. "Wild oranges, they were abundant on these hills."

"I think they are extinct in Jamaica now," Eve said, "they

were highly resistant to termites, they were the best wood to use, and it has withstood three hundred years."

"Yes, let me go and get your robe," Eve said, "and a basket to put your clothes in."

She went inside, and he couldn't quite keep his mouth closed.

The women in this century were undoubtedly different. He couldn't get her figure out of his head.

When she returned, she was dressed; she handed him the basket, a towel, and the robe, "Don't stay too long in your wet things."

He wanted to ask her why that was so important to her. He had spent days in wet clothes at sea but did as she said and changed his clothes. The robe was snug and short; he felt like laughing at himself.

Eve took his clothes and threw them in the dryer. It wasn't his first time seeing the instrument, but as usual, it fascinated him.

"Can we drink the whisky at room temperature, or do we need ice?" she asked.

She placed two glasses on the center table and the whisky between them. "I want to know how three-hundred-year-old whisky tastes," she said.

"Well," Winter said, "I suppose we'll find out soon enough. As for the temperature, it's often said that room temperature allows for the full flavor profile of the whisky to come through, but ultimately, it's a matter of personal preference. Some prefer it chilled, while others enjoy it neat."

Eve nodded, pouring a generous measure of the aged whisky into each glass. As she handed one to Winter, their fingers brushed briefly, sending a subtle jolt of electricity through him.

He took a moment to savor the aroma rising from the glass,

the rich and complex scent hinting at the oak barrels they were stored in before being bottled and centuries of aging. Raising his glass to Eve, Winter offered a small smile.

"To new experiences," he said, clinking his glass gently against hers before taking a sip. The whisky enveloped his senses with its warmth, the smoothness of the liquid sliding down his throat like liquid gold.

He closed his eyes, allowing himself to be fully present in the moment, savoring the taste of history and tradition that lingered on his tongue.

Eve watched him, her glass poised at her lips as she waited for his reaction. Winter opened his eyes to meet her gaze, a soft smile on his lips.

"It's exquisite," he said, his voice barely above a whisper. "It reminds me of home. Whiskey is indeed better when it's older."

Eve imitated him and immediately began to cough.

"It's not bad. It tastes like what I imagine old wood would taste like if it were liquified."

Winter chuckled at her reaction, amused by her candidness. I suppose it's an acquired taste," he said, taking another sip of the whisky to hide his grin. "But you're right. There's something about the aged oak barrels that gives the whisky its unique flavor."

Eve nodded, recovering from her coughing fit with a sheepish smile. "I can see the appeal," she admitted, setting her glass on the table. "Though I'll stick to my usual wine for now."

They sat in comfortable silence for a moment, and then Winter's eyes caught the desk. "There is the desk that was in my room." He got up and sat down before it. "It has a secret compartment, did you know?"

"No," Eve said, "I don't use it except as a place to rest

my laptop." Winter opened the compartment, and there it was, his diary from 1719 to 1720. He smiled triumphantly. "I found it!"

"Yay, I am happy for you," Eve said. "What are the odds that you would find it in the counting house? This was the very last place you looked." She got up and came over to him. "I am a believer. Read it to me." She turned up the light system in the room, and he stared at it, fascinated.

"The next time I come back, I'm going to find out how these things work," Winter said.

Eve smiled. "Of course."

March 21st 1719

It's almost the new year. Walker's visit has turned out to be enlightening. He escaped England to avoid the avid attention of Lady Sarah Peckham, who insists that Walker marry one of her girls. However, Walker finds none of them attractive. He jokes that not even in his sleep, in a deep, dark room, could he carry out his husbandly duties.

Our father sympathized with his plight and gave him the go-ahead to join me for a while in the colonies. I am quite pleased with my current abode, my house on Crimson Hills.

Walker is obsessed with my timepiece, the sundial. 'What if the legend around it is true?' he asks me daily. 'What if you can traverse the halls of time?'

His incessant questions make me curious. I gather the papers that the shifty man who sold it to me had given me as part of the sale. It says it can only be activated during a vernal equinox.

Tomorrow will be a vernal equinox when the day and the night are equal. I wonder if Walker's curiosity will lead us toward adventure or folly. But at this moment, as the sun sets over Crimson Hills, casting long shadows across the landscape, I am filled with anticipation, eager to uncover the mysteries hidden within the depths of time. I will take Walker up on his dare to traverse the annals of time."

March 29th 1719

I must write this before I forget. Something monumental has happened to me. I can scarcely believe it. On the day of the equinox, when the shadow on the sundial was an exact straight line, I turned the sundial 200 degrees in the middle. Before the equinox, no one could shift the needle in the middle. It was as if the equinox was a key to unlock the device.

I chose two hundred degrees because of a simple math equation. If the Bible character, Hezekiah, got 15 years at 10 degrees, I could move forward to 300 years at 200 degrees.

It was an experiment, and it worked. I felt myself slipping. It was a sensation akin to falling off a cliff.

Walker stood before me, and he faded away. The clouds overhead switched to night and then to day again in rapid succession. Then, I was standing beside the same sundial but feeling greatly dizzy. I looked around. The landscape had changed. The overgrown grass and woodlands were neatly arranged, and there were subtle, unexpected changes, too numerous to name.

A woman, slim and dressed in strange clothing— a white top and a red and white skirt that looked full and long— was walking by when she stopped abruptly. Whatever she was carrying in her hand fell, and she stood still, blinking rapidly at me.

I approached her and asked, "What century is this?"

"The twenty-first," she whispered.

"What year?"

"Twenty-nineteen."

"The Great House is not open for visitors due to COVID-19 protocols," she said.

I barely heard what she said. A black man carrying what looked like a sword came around the corner and stopped. I later learned that his weapon was a machete, a tool, not an instrument for war.

"That's my husband, Willie Beecher," the woman said, "and I am Maud. We are the caretakers here; we live in the carriage house."

"The carriage house?" I whispered, feeling off-kilter.

"Maybe you should come inside and sit down," Maud suggested.

I headed for the front door, and she hurriedly opened it for me, stepping aside.

I sat down in the nearest chair. "I don't think you will believe me," I whispered, "but I am…"

"Winter Wesson," Maud said. "Your portrait is over there."

I looked up, and there was my portrait. I had commissioned it to be done, but I had yet to pose for it.

I learned several things about this century in the month I stayed here. The differences were astounding. My brother, Walker, and I speculated about the future, but this was beyond my imagination. The twenty-first century is a place of wonder, with electricity at your fingertips, transportation that defies belief, and communication beyond comprehension. It's a world where information flows freely, where knowledge is accessible with a few keystrokes. Yet, it's also a world fraught with challenges and complexities, where the pace of life seems to move faster than ever before.

I spent my days in awe, exploring this new era and trying to understand its customs and technologies. Maud and

Willie were gracious hosts, patiently answering my endless questions and guiding me through this unfamiliar landscape.

But as the days passed, a longing grew within me, a longing for home, for the familiar comforts of my own time. I realized that as miraculous as this journey had been, it was not where I belonged.

And so, on the morning of April 25th, exactly one month after my arrival, I stood before the sundial again, ready to return to my own time. With a deep breath and a prayer on my lips, I tried to turn the dial back 200 degrees, but it would not budge.

I walked toward the blurry, unfocused trees beyond the gates of the great house. Since I could not go back, I decided to explore. But as soon as I stepped through the gate and into the other side, I was back in 1719. I was almost run down by my brother's horse.

He was frantic with worry. He said he saw me disappear right before him. Cornelius, my manservant, had been standing on the steps of the great house; he said he saw it too. I had much to tell them about my time travel experience.

****

"Wow," Eve whispered, "just wow."

Walker looked up from the ledger. "The second time I traveled was much less dramatic. I knew what to expect. My only grievance with the sundial was that it would not budge from the 200 degrees I had it on initially. It seems I can only come back to this time."

Eve nodded.

"And then I met you and began to wonder if more than coincidence is involved here. I feel like I know you, as if somehow you are my fate."

"I feel the same way," Eve whispered. "It is scary and thrilling at the same time."

Winter smiled. "I am going to skip through to this year. I am anxious to know how I saved my brother."

She nodded. "Read on."

Chapter Twelve

September 8, 1720

We rode out at dusk. The harbor master sent word that Murdock Bartholomew had passed close by just that afternoon. His ship was headed for Negril, just off the coast of Lignum Bay, marked by a grove of sea grapes where he docks. There is a shanty tavern made from bamboo that was erected in a large clearing where pirates and their cronies went to drink. Murdock and his twelve men dock there. Two men are left on the boat with the prisoners, Wesley and two other boys of noble families. I was nervous for Wesley; what shape was he in?

We approached three ships, Walker, Cornelius, and I, along with some pirate hunters and two other frigates alongside ours. The salty breeze whipped through our hair as we drew nearer to the shanty tavern, its silhouette growing more defined against the fading hues of the evening sky.

The crew's chatter and the ships' creaking melded with the waves' rhythm, creating a symphony of anticipation.

As we anchored near the grove of sea grapes, the air became tense. Murdock Bartholomew's reputation preceded him, and every man aboard was keenly aware of the risks involved in confronting him and his band of pirates. Yet, duty compelled us forward, our resolve bolstered by the thought of rescuing Wesley and the other captives.

Our ships positioned themselves strategically with practiced precision, flanking the tavern from different angles. The moon cast an eerie glow upon the scene, illuminating the makeshift structure and the figures milling about its perimeter.

I gripped the railing, my pulse quickening with each passing moment. The fate of Wesley and the other boys weighed heavily on my mind as we prepared to confront the notorious pirate and his crew. This was no ordinary skirmish; it was a clash of wills, a test of courage and cunning.

As we readied ourselves for the impending confrontation, I wondered what awaited us within the dimly lit confines of the tavern. We need not have worried; Murdock and his men were three sheets to the wind. It was an easy takedown.

****

"You got him!" Eve squealed. "That's great!"

Winter nodded. "We got him. I will have to return to my time with this information."

Eve nodded. "But you have time, didn't you say it was September 8? We are just in July."

"No," Winter shook his head. My September is your July. Our year starts in March, and yours starts in January. Our calendars do not synchronize, even with the variations in the placement of the months. I am going to have to leave tonight. The longer I tarry here, the less likely I am to save my brother."

"But you just got here," Eve whispered, "and you haven't told me what 'three sheets to the wind' means."

Winter laughed. "The sheet is the line that controls the sails on a ship. If the line is not secured, the sail flops in the wind, and the ship loses headway and control. If all three sails are loose, the ship is out of control. Murdock and his crew were thoroughly drunk, so much so that they could barely stand. They were in no state to put up a fight, making our task considerably easier."

"Oh," Eve said, "it's a ship term."

Winter nodded, "One, I assume, is outdated now."

"I am sure people use it," Eve said, "but I have never heard it."

"I must go," Winter said, his tone resolute yet tinged with regret. "Time is of the essence, and I cannot afford to delay any longer."

Eve nodded. Her expression was filled with understanding. "I'll miss you," she whispered.

Winter's gaze softened as he reached out to clasp her hand. "I'll miss you too," he murmured, his words laden with unspoken emotion. "But I'll return, I promise."

"When?" Eve asked.

"At our next vernal equinox, which is March."

"But I needed more time with you," Eve whispered.

Winter moved closer; her face was so close to his, he could place his lips on hers.

She moved even closer. "Tell me something. Do they kiss in the 1700s? I mean, what's the practice?"

Winter's heart quickened at the proximity of Eve's face to his, her warm breath mingling with his own. He could feel the tension crackling between them, a palpable energy that seemed to draw them closer with each passing moment.

"In the 1700s," Winter began, his voice barely above a whisper, "the practice of kissing was not as openly displayed as it is today. It was often reserved for more intimate moments between lovers, and even then, it was considered somewhat scandalous in certain circles."

Eve's gaze remained fixed on his, her lips tantalizingly close to his own.

"But that doesn't mean it didn't happen," Winter continued, his voice growing husky with desire. "In private, away from prying eyes, couples would steal moments together, exchanging kisses as a symbol of affection and passion. I want to kiss you all over."

As he spoke, Winter felt a surge of boldness coursing through him, fueled by his undeniable attraction to Eve. Without another word, he closed the distance between them, kissing her lips tenderly.

Time seemed to stand still as their lips met, a rush of warmth flooding through Winter's veins at the contact. At that moment, there was only the sensation of Eve's lips against his own, the softness of her touch igniting a fire within him that he couldn't ignore.

He did not want to let her go.

When they finally pulled away, their breaths coming in ragged gasps, Winter found himself lost in the depths of Eve's eyes, his heart pounding in his chest. "I suppose some practices never truly go out of style," he murmured, a smile tugging at the corners of his lips.

Eve smiled back, her eyes shining with amusement and desire. "Indeed," she replied, her voice barely above a whisper.

"I will see you soon," Winter whispered. "Expect a note

from me weekly until then."

"Where?" Eve asked.

"In the desk's secret compartment, I'll show you how to access it."

Eve smiled. "Your notes won't be weekly for me; I'd be reading them all at once."

"That's right," Winter smiled, "I never thought of that."

Chapter Thirteen

Eve snapped back to the present day.

She had stood in the drizzling rain and watched Winter walk through the great house gates and disappear into thin air. She had even run after him, but all she could see was the palm trees and streetlights on the other side of the road.

She had been morose ever since. Only the notes that Winter had written to her had kept her going. She had read and re-read them. His last entry still burned in her mind.

My dearest Eve,

Sometimes, I feel as if all of this is but a dream. An occasion of happenstance, a whisper in the night, a fleeting touch of destiny's hand upon our lives. Yet, with each passing day, I am more convinced that our connection is more than mere happenstance. It's as if the universe conspires to intertwine our fates and bring us closer despite the chasms of distance and time that separate us.

In the quiet moments when I am alone with my thoughts, I wonder about the mysteries that bind us. What forces propel us toward each other, defying logic and reason? Are the echoes of our shared past and lives lived long ago resonating within our souls? Or is it something more profound, something beyond the grasp of mortal understanding?

Whatever the answer, I find solace in the knowledge that you are out there, somewhere, feeling the same pull that tugs at my heartstrings. And though we may be separated by miles and time, know that you are never far from my thoughts, my dearest Eve.

Until we meet again, in this life or the next,

Winter

Stuart was sitting at Maud's table in the carriage house when she arrived. Stuart had a pleasant face; he seemed to always be on the verge of laughter. He was cute instead of handsome. His thick brown hair, sprinkled with grey, was always boyishly unkempt, and his light brown eyes always had a twinkle.

He was a Wesson through his mother's side of the family. Only a Wesson could head the board of trustees. And he was certainly qualified. He was a business professor at a university in Kingston, but he was very hands-on with the running of the board.

"Hello, Eve," he greeted her cheerily. You are so privileged to live in the same place as Maud. She has homemade bread and butter, cream, chocolate, and the most heavenly green bananas and ackee and saltfish—they melt in your mouth."

Eve sat down. "Can you hit me with something to wake me up, Maud?"

Maud nodded, "Green tea coming right up."

'What have I been hearing about Winter Wesson doing a video for Garnet Silver?"

"Her name is now Knight Hastings," Maud said. "They got married at Knightsbridge; it was the most beautiful wedding I have ever attended."

"Why didn't anyone alert me?" Stuart asked. "Why didn't Winter contact the board? It's his board."

Eve cleared her throat. "Well, it has to do with the sundial. Time travel. I thought it would stretch the limits of your imagination. I did tell him to contact you, but he said he was only staying long enough to find his diary. He wanted to rescue his brother from a pirate named Murdock."

Eve watched to see if Stuart would laugh heartily, but he didn't.

"Someone should have told me," Stuart said. "A part of the protocol for being head of the board of trustees is to prepare for Winter Wesson's return. I have always thought it was ridiculous. But here we are. It is in our bylaws."

Maud laughed and clapped her hands. "That man is smart. Haven't I always said he is different?"

Eve was stunned. "What's the wording for that exactly?"

"It is quite specific," Stuart said. "It is long and detailed, but basically, it says that in the event of Winter Wesson's reappearance in the twenty-first century, the head of the board of trustees is to ensure that all necessary preparations are made to accommodate his return, including but not limited to providing assistance in adjusting to the modern world and his integration back into society. We were to anticipate his needs for identification, etc.

"We are to repossess the old Rafferty house if it comes up for sale. He doesn't want to live in a showroom house."

"Apparently, the great house is a showroom house," Maud

said.

"Oh my goodness," Eve muttered. "I told him that."

Maud served her tea and sat down.

"Strangely, it makes sense," Stuart said. "You might as well know, Eve. You were also in our bylaws. We were supposed to get your services by any means necessary by 2016. So we contacted your father and allowed things to flow from there."

Eve sipped the tea; the hot liquid burned her tongue. "That's amazing!"

"He arranged it," Maud said.

"Apparently." Stuart cleared his throat. "Another aspect of our bylaws is that we should find an expert for the sundial. Somebody who would know how it operates. The board of trustees, since the 1700s, have always sent out feelers to find out who would be an expert.

"We recently found someone quite by chance. We saw him in a documentary discussing ancient artifacts. His name is Isaac Stein, a Jewish historian who currently lives in Britain.

"We already invited him to come and check out the sundial. He said he would be here in January but had to cancel; unforeseen events caused a delay. I should tell him it's a matter of urgency. I am sure he will drop everything to come and see our time traveler when Winter comes back."

"Nobody will believe this," Eve whispered.

"I can believe it," Maud said. "After I read that poem he wrote about you, I knew that man wouldn't give you up. I knew he'd plan to stay with you in this century."

"What poem?" Eve asked.

"It was entitled Winter's Eve. I gave it to him when he was here the last time." Maud said. "It's his, after all. If he wanted you to know about it, he'd give it to you."

"Oh, he mentioned that," Eve said. "I never followed up with him. So much has been happening."

"It's too bad Winter is coming when I am going to guest lecture at a university in Florida for four weeks. Do you think he will still be here when I get back?"

"I have no clue," Eve said. "He doesn't stay for long."

"No, he doesn't," Maud said. "The first time he spent a week, the second time he spent two, and the third time he just came for the diary to see where Wesley was taken."

"It just hit me that you are related to Winter. It must be exciting to see someone from so far up on your family tree."

"It is," Stuart chuckled. "I would cancel the lecture and wait to see him. But I got myself locked in and it's too late to find a replacement."

"Do you know how you two are related?" Eve asked. "Can you trace the lineage?"

"Of course," Stuart nodded. "It's a thing of pride for us Wessons to do. It is easy to trace because of the trust. Only people with a direct line to Winter are eligible as beneficiaries, so through the years, the trust has kept strict tabs on who is who. We have our own ancestry register. It will be awesome to meet the man whose trust has helped thousands, not just his immediate family."

Chapter Fourteen

The sadness she had been battling since Winter left suddenly lifted. She didn't know how they would work out a relationship between them when they lived in different centuries. She didn't know what the solution would be, but March was approaching, and she felt he was coming back. She was on a euphoric high for days. She went to visit her mother at work for lunch. If she were to tell her parents, they wouldn't believe her. But she was going to burst if she didn't tell someone.

"You seem to be happy, dear," Veronica said. "It's a good change from the grumpiness I've seen you with these last few months."

"And there was a reason for that," Eve said excitedly. They were sitting in the café at her parents' building. It was a popular eatery for the real estate section and law firm staff, so it probably wasn't the best place to blurt out the reason for her happiness.

"I am in a long-distance relationship, and he is returning soon."

"Ah, I knew there was a man," her mother smiled. "I saw how different you were at the gala last year; you were glowing. I assumed you had a breakup with how you acted these last couple of months, but it turns out it was just a long-distance situation. When can we meet him?"

"I don't know if he can leave the great house," Eve mused.

Her mother frowned. "I thought this was a long-distance relationship? Where's the distance if he is at the great house?"

"He is at the great house at a different time," Eve said. "We are separated by time, not distance."

Her mother leaned closer. "Honey, it is okay if you don't want to tell me about this relationship. I will not interfere. Your father and I insisted on you marrying David and look how that turned out. We will not poke our nosy selves into any future relationship you have. I feel a certain burden that I am partially responsible for your unhappiness these last few years. I will never insist on a marriage before you are ready."

"Mom," Eve sighed, "I knew telling you this would blow your mind."

"You can tell me anything, dear," her mother said. "I am unshockable. I have been practicing criminal law for thirty years."

"I fell in love with Winter Wesson," Eve said. "The original Winter Wesson."

"Okay, fine, I would like to meet him."

"Are you taking me seriously?" Eve asked.

"Quite so," Veronica nodded. "I would like to meet him before I become further concerned about your mental health."

Eve laughed. "I knew your response was too calm. He should be coming back soon, and you must come to the great house to meet him. He cannot leave the confines of the place."

"Sure," her mother nodded. "I'll visit. Let me know when."

Veronica's phone rang before she could say anything further; she answered.

"Honey, I have to go. There is a break in a current case I am working on. Sorry to cut our lunch short, but I don't care who is making you happy, whether he is from this time or the past. I love it when you are happy."

She kissed Eve and walked away.

"There was no way she could be that calm about what she just heard; she was probably preoccupied with something else," Eve thought.

She finished her lunch, scrolling through her phone as she tried to find any new information on the Wesson family. Their Crimson Hill Great House website had the most comprehensive history, but there was nothing new.

Instead, she turned to the ancient artifacts documentary Stuart had told her about and found Dr. Isaac Stein.

The introduction to the program said:

"Many ancient artifacts, found worldwide, hold profound mysteries and stories waiting to be unraveled. Dr. Isaac Stein, a renowned archaeologist, has dedicated his life to exploring these enigmatic relics, shedding light on lost civilizations and forgotten cultures. From the towering pyramids of Egypt to the hidden temples of South America, each artifact unearthed by Dr. Stein unveiled a piece of humanity's rich tapestry, revealing tantalizing clues about our collective past. Today, he will shed some light on the time travel device known as Hezekiah's sundial.

The Bible recorded that King Hezekiah of Judah

experienced a miraculous event involving a sundial. According to the biblical account in the book of 2 Kings, Chapter 20, verses 8-11, King Hezekiah fell ill. He was told by the prophet Isaiah that he would die. Hezekiah prayed to God, and as a sign that his life would be extended, he asked for the shadow on the sundial to move backward ten steps. Where is that sundial today, and does it still work? Was it mentioned in the Bible as the only account of time travel?"

Dr. Stein came on the screen; he was a slim-bodied, bookish-looking man with wild hair.

"We are still uncovering information from our site in Egypt. We made a huge haul from a little-known library, which we have dated to be at least 4000 years BCE. Thankfully, the technology is around to decipher what is on the papyrus we discovered in this ancient library. Our attempts to open these scripts manually have resulted in their degradation. So we have to use special technology to view what's on them without touching it.

"A few notable texts we have discovered thus far mention a time-travel device in the form of a sundial. According to the texts, four of them were created. The texts describe how they work and their capabilities.

"According to the texts, powerful magnetite crystals were embedded in the base of the time device. These crystals worked in tandem with the Earth's magnetic force, which seems to be stronger at certain times of the year, usually at the equinox.

"It is interesting to note that the human brain contains magnetite crystals, a fairly recent discovery. However, the ancient texts mention that the crystals in the body correspond with the crystals in the device.

"This means that the device will only respond to the person who activates it. So, apparently, there can be only one user at a time. When a person time travels, the device provides a protective cloak around the area like a shield. I assume it's to limit the pollution of the timeline.

"It is an exciting piece of technology, but it does have some drawbacks. The person who travels cannot use it too often. There are cautionary tales of frequent use, causing the user to disappear in time and disintegrate."

Eve gasped. How many times had Winter traveled so far? And didn't his history say he disappeared in 1721? She half listened to the rest of Dr. Stein's interview and then perked up when he said,

"Yes, time travel is possible, according to these ancient texts, but is it safe?" Dr. Stein asked, "That is up for debate."

She put down the phone as if it had burned her.

"Earth to Eve," David stood before her. "You look like you have seen a ghost."

"I just heard something unpleasant," Eve said. "What's up?"

"You haven't answered my texts or emails," David said. "I am really interested in buying the house."

"Oh," Eve said, "sorry about that. I may have blocked you in anger a couple of years ago on all my devices."

David sat down. "Eve, you are still not over me, are you?"

"I am," Eve nodded. "I am so over you. I haven't thought about you in months. I am not even angry with you anymore. I am grateful that we are no longer together. It was a good and wise choice to divorce me. And yes, I'll sell you the house. You'll have to talk to my dad about it, though. I asked him to handle the sale."

David looked at her in amazement. "Well, uh, thank you."

"No problem," Eve said.

Winter was in trouble, she thought feverishly. He was going to disappear in 1721.

David leaned forward, frightening her; she hadn't realized he was still there; she had completely blocked him out.

"It's okay if you still have feelings for me," he said. "I do sometimes think about you too. I may have ended things too early."

"What?" Eve frowned.

"You are so beautiful," David said, admiring her. "I may have made a mistake in letting you go."

"Oh, David," Eve sighed, "my interest in hearing you say things like that is way below zero."

"Are you seeing anyone?" David asked.

"Yes," Eve nodded, "And I love him."

"I don't believe you," David said.

"I don't care," Eve said, "does Tiffany know you are propositioning other women? Why aren't you two married yet? I thought you were engaged."

"I realized she is not my one true love," David shrugged, "we called it quits a month ago."

"Oh my," Eve said, "I am truly sorry to hear that you wasted so much of her time. But she should have seen it coming. You are a two-year man. You can't keep a relationship for longer than that."

"I am not a two-year man," David grimaced. "I really thought she was the one. Maybe it was you, after all."

Eve shook her head in disbelief. "David, I've moved on, I have no interest in you whatsoever. If I did, I would beat myself or hire someone to do it for me. I'd have them use a heavy belt or maybe ropes. And I would deserve the beating because I would have a punishment kink to even think of having a relationship with you again."

"I get the message, Eve," David shrugged. "I won't bother you again."

"Here's a piece of advice," Eve said. "It's free. In your

next relationship, tell her upfront about your two-year limit. If she is fine with it, then good, but don't pretend that you want a long-term commitment with anyone; you don't. It's just not in you."

She got up. "I have to go. I have more pressing matters to deal with."

Chapter Fifteen

Winter walked through the gate and into the hazy blur of the other side. Of course, he knew that doing so would bring him to his century.

"Ahoy there, Lord Wesson!" the sentry greeted him jovially.

"Ahoy there, August."

"We just got word from the harbor master that Murdock was spotted earlier this morning," August said.

"So he had come at the right time," Winter nodded. "Thank you, August."

He stood back and looked at the house; it always struck him what a difference three hundred years made to it.

In this time, it was brand new. He took in the differences in the landscape. The flowers and the manicured lawns were all gone. Where they parked their modern vehicles was now filled with horses. Many more horses than he was used to having on the hills.

And there were several riders with them.

Walker appeared at the top steps of the great house and saw him. His face lit up. "You're back!"

"I am back," Winter said. "Who are these people?"

"Pirate hunters. I got them together so we could head on out by the time you arrived. This has been the longest week of my life."

Winter hugged his brother fondly and clapped him on the shoulder. "You were so confident that I would have gotten the information," he said.

"You said they knew everything about us in the twenty-first century," Walker said.

"It turns out they don't, but my writings about the events enlightened me. Aren't you happy that I write down everything?"

"I am. What did you learn this time?" Walker asked.

"Murdock is drinking at a watering hole off the coast of Negril. At precisely 9:23 pm tonight, he and his men are so drunk we can easily tie them together."

Walker rubbed his hands together. "Good."

"We rescue Wesley, who is a little worse for wear, but he'll survive. He lives up to the ripe old age of ninety-nine."

"Ninety-nine!" Walker guffawed. "He has eighty-three more years to go?"

"He does," Winter nodded. "I think his lifestyle as a scholar may have something to do with that. When father is gone, he will stay here at Crimson Hills until his death, living the life of a gentleman author."

"How long will I live?" Walker asked. "And what took me out?"

"You die fifty years from now in Britain. You are the Duke of Wesson," Winter said. "The records did not say how you died."

"What?" Walker asked, shocked. "What happened to Willhelm? He didn't make it."

"No," Winter said. "You know he drinks like a fish; his death was caused by alcohol poisoning. Father went a few months before him, a heart attack."

"Why am I the Duke of Wesson? You are the spare, not me. I have never wanted that responsibility."

"There is no record of my death," Winter said. "I seem to have disappeared in 1721. There are no records of me anywhere."

"Are you sure you didn't just chicken out of the duke role?"

"I am not sure," Winter said. "I have no idea what will happen to me in 1721."

"Whatever it is, it's not good," Walker said. "I don't want to be the next Duke of Wesson. The title anchors you to England and curtails future adventure."

"You will be fine," Winter said, "you look a lot like Dad in your portrait."

"What else have you learned?" Walker asked.

"I'd rather not say," Winter said, "time will unfold soon enough."

"You are right," Walker nodded, "besides, we have plenty of time to come to terms with our respective futures."

****

They rode out at dusk. The pirate hunters had yet to ask many questions. He just told them the time and the location. He and Walker would take their own ship to carry Wesley home. Their manservant, Cornelius, accompanied them.

"What was it like this time?" Cornelius asked.

Winter stood on the dock as the men prepped their ship. Nearby, other ships were unloading cargo, even at this late hour. Some of the cargo were people, mostly black people. He spotted a few Native Indians with them, all tied together with chains. There were ten slaves to every white man.

"I met a girl, a woman. I love her."

"Oh really?" Cornelius raised his eyebrows. "That's going to pose a problem. You live three hundred years in her past."

"It doesn't have to be a problem," Winter said. "I can move easily between times, from one vernal equinox to another."

"What if she is a relative? You said you can't leave the great house grounds while you are there."

"That's true," Winter nodded. "I doubt she is a relative; even if she is, she would be several generations removed from me. Besides, she is fully black; I don't think the lineage has changed that much."

"Oh my," Cornelius whispered, "so it's a forbidden relationship."

"It's not forbidden in the twenty-first century to marry someone of a different shade. The difference between you and me, Cornelius, is cosmetic. You have more melanin than I do; that is all. I hate the notion that we are of different races. We are one race; we are both human."

"If only more people thought like you," Cornelius said, "then slavery would not be a thing. Your people justify slavery by calling us a different race."

"I know," Winter nodded. "As I've said to you many times, it does get better. Three hundred years from now, the descendants of slaves are the ones who run this country, your people are free and slavery is a relic of our times."

Cornelius inhaled. "That's good to know. Every time you say it, it gives me hope."

Winter nodded.

****

They amassed at Negril point, just as he had written. Murdock and his men were like putty in their hands. They found Wesley tied up, dehydrated, and half-starved. It took his brother weeks to recover.

"I am leaving at the next equinox. My journal indicates that I will disappear in 1721," Winter said.

Wesley nodded listlessly. "I am going to lose everyone."

"No, you won't," Winter said. "I am going to lose everyone shortly. You will have your wife and children to keep you company. You'll be happy writing your books. I, on the other hand, disappear into thin air."

Wesley's eyes lit up. "I am a writer?"

Winter nodded. "A famous one."

Wesley laughed heartily.

"You will tell Arthur of me," Winter said. You will be responsible for keeping my legacy alive. I will set up a board of trustees; you will run it, and you will see to it that every successive board knows of their mission: to keep the Wesson legacy alive."

"I will do so, brother. You can count on me."

As the months drifted in and out. Winter yearned to go back to Eve.

"I will stay longer this time," he told his brothers. "At least three months. I am going to ask her to marry me."

"That's preposterous, brother," Walker protested. "You cannot be an eighteenth-century groom to a twenty-first-century bride."

"But I disappear a year from now," Winter said. "I think I should live as fully as I can."

Chapter Sixteen

Eve opened her door. It was one of those cloudy days, and she lacked her usual enthusiasm to go to work, but she had a conference call with the board of trustees. She bit back a yelp. Winter was fast asleep on her veranda. He must have sensed her presence. He opened his eyes. His beautiful green eyes.

"I missed you so much," Eve said, crouching to his level and hugging him close. "I can't tell you how much."

"I missed you more, My Eve," he whispered in her sweet-smelling hair.

"This has to be your last travel," Eve said urgently. "Going back and forth with the sundial will kill you."

Winter smiled. "So, in other words, you want me to stay with you?"

"Forever," Eve said. "But I am serious; there are side effects to your time traveling. I'll leave you with a video to watch for yourself. I'd watch it with you, but I have to go. I have a virtual meeting in five minutes. Stuart is in Florida, and he has strict meeting times. I don't want to be late. By the way, the last couple of months have been hell." She kissed him soundly. "I'll tell Maud you are here."

Winter watched Eve leave, feeling torn between his desire to stay with her and his sense of duty to tie up loose ends in his own time. He knew he had to go back one final time. Luckily, he didn't have to worry about traveling again until September, six months away. He settled into a chair on the veranda and reached for the tablet Eve had left behind. He began watching the video of Isaac Stein explaining the sundial and its potential effects on time travelers.

Should he take the chance on another trip to the eighteenth century? Would that be his last trip? Lost in thought, Winter pondered his next steps. He had been so eager to be back here with Eve that he had not considered that there would be consequences of him traversing the centuries so casually. But if he never went back, he wouldn't see Walker again, and he wouldn't be able to make arrangements for life in this century. Besides, would four trips really be thought of as abuse?

"I heard you were back!" Maud said excitedly.

Winter smiled. "I am back."

"Are you hungry?" Maud asked.

"Famished," Winter said, realizing he was.

"I just learned that time traveling regularly has negative consequences," Winter said, shaking his head. "If I go back and wait for the next equinox, I will disappear."

"How?" Maud asked.

"Maybe I spontaneously combust. I don't know," Winter fretted. "You watched the video; the man said people disappear."

"It hasn't happened yet. No need to worry about it," Maud

said. "You came back for Eve, didn't you?"

Winter nodded.

"Then live like the time you have together is precious and cherish every moment," Maud finished for him, placing a reassuring hand on his shoulder. "Make the most of the present."

"You're right," Winter nodded. "I can't let fear of the unknown dictate my actions. I returned for Eve, and I'll make sure every second counts."

Maud smiled softly. "That's the spirit. And who knows, maybe the future isn't as grim as you imagine. But regardless, focusing on the here and now is what truly matters."

****

April flew by like it was on steroids, and to make every day count, he spent every waking moment with Eve. He had a lot to learn about the twenty-first century. Eve bought him his first laptop, and he researched to his heart's content in the days while she worked. They had lunch together at various spots on the Great House property and dinner mostly every night.

"I wish I could show you this country properly," Eve said. "The things we could do, the places we would go."

It was the weekend, and they were lounging under a cotton tree. He knew this particular tree from his time. It looked the same to him. The sunlight filtered through the leaves, casting dappled patterns on the ground, and a stream trickled nearby. Winter leaned back against the trunk, feeling the warmth of Eve's presence beside him.

"It's okay, Eve," he said softly, reaching for her hand. "Just being with you like this is enough for me. I don't need to see every corner of the country to appreciate what we have."

Eve smiled, gently squeezing his hand. "You're too sweet, Winter. But I want you to experience everything this world has to offer. We'll find a way. If you stay here, you must stay at the great house forever. That's no way to live."

"I agree," Winter said, "but I don't want to leave you. I will have to decide: your century or mine, live with you trapped in the great house or live free in my time, thinking about you, trapped in my emotions."

"You'd forget me and move on," Eve inhaled. "Time, they say, heals all wounds."

"And you would recover and find another," Winter looked at her, frowning. "Alas, my love, you do me wrong, To cast me off discourteously, For I have loved you well and long, Delighting in your company."

Eve laughed. "That's not your poem, Winter Wesson, that's Greensleeves. We play it here to enhance the authenticity of the tour."

"It's an old song," Winter said, "even in my day."

"So, what are some of the hip modern songs in the 1700s then?" Eve asked.

Winter readily listed the songs: "Black-Eyed Susan, The Vicar of Bray, The Vicar, and Moses, Pretty Polly Oliver."

"Oh," Eve grinned, "I thought the people in your century only listened to instrumentals like Bach and Vivaldi."

"We had popular music too; we are the same people, just limited by technology and practices," Winter said. "I theorize that we have more things in common because we are the same human beings with the same nature."

"I hear you," Eve nodded. "People will be people; we just find more sophisticated ways to do our peopling."

Winter chuckled. "Peopling?"

"I don't know if it's a word. Maybe it was a word in your time."

"I don't know of it," Winter said.

"Tell me more about the music," Eve said. "Did you have love songs?"

"The song Pretty Polly Oliver tells of a young woman who disguises herself as a man to join her lover in the army. It's a tale of love, adventure, and the willingness to defy societal norms for the sake of love."

"Aw, that sounds cool," Eve said. "And you liked it?"

"I liked the message," Winter said, "I've always been a little before my time where gender and race issues are concerned. My mother's influence, I suppose. She didn't fit in, and she ensured that we saw the hypocrisy in the societal norms of our time. So, I appreciate stories that challenge those norms and celebrate love and courage in all its forms."

Eve smiled. "When you say things like that, I love you even more."

Winter kissed her at the top of her head.

"I want us to have a happy ending," Eve murmured. "And I have to constantly remind myself to live in the moment. The way I feel about you, I would probably be OK going to live in the 1700s."

"I would never ask you to choose to live with me in my time," Winter said. "We could not marry, and our children would not be acknowledged as legitimate. It is an unequal world, as you pointed out before. But Eve, I have to go back; I haven't put anything in place to ensure this future that we are now enjoying."

"What do you mean?" Eve asked.

"I have no plan for a board of trustees, I have not put aside any provisions for me to live here, and I have not told my brothers or sons goodbye. I need to set things in order before I disappear."

He took a tendril of her hair and tucked it behind her ear.

"Is it wrong of me to think of marrying you right now? Would it even be right if I disappear in a few months?"

"I think we should live in the present; our future will work things out," Eve said.

"Then let's get married," Winter said.

"We can't be legally married unless you want us to have a symbolic marriage," Eve whispered.

"Why can't we be legally married?" Winter asked.

"We'd need legal documents, like a birth certificate," Eve said.

Winter nodded, "Okay, I'll get it."

"I don't think it's that easy," Eve said. "Well, I really have no clue. We should ask Stuart. He'll be here on Monday. He is dying to meet you. Once you get a birth certificate, we can discuss getting married. I am not sure that I want to be rushed into a second marriage."

"That's fair," Winter nodded. "I am going to tackle the writing of the trustee agreement. Based on what I have seen and heard, and being privy to the future, I know what to write."

Chapter Seventeen

"**H**oney, I am coming to your office for lunch," Veronica called Eve the following Monday. "Your father and I are concerned."

"About what, Mom?" Eve asked absently; she had a pile of work to do. There was an event at the great house the next day, a fussy bride who wanted an eighteenth-century aesthetic for her wedding. Both the bride and groom would be getting ready in the great house to lend to the authenticity. The couple had booked the great house for the day to take pre-wedding photos. Eve was summoned every five minutes by a frustrated Maud, who had to tell the wedding party to stick to their agreed-upon use of the facilities. Besides, Stuart was going to arrive any minute now. Winter was sitting at her assistant's desk, looking like a modern-day movie star dressed all in black. He looked across at her and winked.

"Mom," Eve cleared her throat. "This is not a good time."

"Why?" Veronica asked. "Because you are hanging out with your 1700s boyfriend? Eve, I said I would not interfere, but I have to. You haven't visited us in a month. Your so-called boyfriend cannot leave the great house because he is a time traveler constrained by his time machine, a sundial. Honey, do you know how ridiculous this sounds?"

"Yes," Eve said, "but I can assure you I am operating in my right mind. I am actually quite busy today."

"I am not buying it," Veronica said. "It sounds as if you are keeping me at arm's length. I am coming up there with food. I will be there at twelve-thirty. Is curry goat from Norman's okay?"

"It's fine," Eve grumbled. "I should be done with the meeting by then, but it can't be a long lunch. I have some problem guests."

"Okay," Veronica said.

Winter came over to her desk and handed her a note. "I wrote this while you were grumpily answering your phone calls."

Eve chuckled. He wrote her poems every day. She opened the paper and read:

"My heart glows when you smile,
A radiant beam, so warm and beguile.
In your laughter, I find my peace,
As if all the world's worries cease."

Eve smiled. "Ah, thank you, Winter. I wish I were poetic, but I am not creatively inclined."

"I am quite content to be the poetic one in our relationship," Winter said. "When I return to my timeline, I intend to write you a poem every day until I return."

"That would be reassuring," Eve said, "since you insist on

returning."

"You know I have to," Winter said. "Or this place may just end up being a crumbled ruin like so many other great houses in this country. I have been reading up on them. There are not that many left."

"True," Eve nodded.

"Without the trust, there is no controlling the wealth for generations to come. Besides, you wouldn't be working here. I would not have met you. What's the use of coming back here if we don't meet? I have started outlining some of the things that I want to be carried out. I want free-to-attend science-based school, a fund for scientific thinkers to finance their projects to advance the world and to reward the curious, the outside-the-box thinkers."

"It sounds like you're getting along quite fine," Eve smiled.

"When did you start working here?" Winter asked.

"Twenty-sixteen," Eve said.

"And what's the name of your father's business?"

"Wait a minute," Eve said, stunned. "You did outline that I should be contacted in your trustee agreement."

Winter smiled. "So I might know how to write an agreement after all, with some help from the internet, too. Tell me, Eve, all about your journey here because I don't want to miss out on meeting you."

****

Stuart entered the office, his brown eyes lighting up. "As I live and breathe, it's you! I know it's possible. I saw that video you did with Garnet Silver, but to see you in the flesh is to believe it."

Winter smiled. "Stuart, it's good to put a face to the voice over the telephone."

Stuart grabbed Winter's hand for a handshake and wouldn't let it go. "It feels real. I am touching my ancestor, the Winter Wesson, who looks much younger than I am."

Winter laughed. "It's the irony of time travel."

Stuart sat in front of Eve. "I thought I was ready for this."

"Take your time," Eve said soothingly. "I guess I didn't react this way because I didn't believe he was the original Winter."

"I brought lunch," her mother said at the door. And then she froze. Eve knew the exact moment that it registered. She had known that her mother had not taken her seriously before, and this confirmed it. Veronica Blair, attorney-at-law, was speechless. It was a sight to see.

"Mom, this is Winter Wesson and Stuart Smithson, the head of the board of trustees."

"Oh," her mother said.

Winter got up, and they shook hands. "It is lovely to meet you, Mrs. Blair."

"Let us leave you to your lunch," Stuart said to Eve. "Winter and I have a lot to discuss."

"Wait a minute," Veronica said. "He's not really the Winter Wesson, is he?"

"I am, my lady," Winter said gallantly.

"But it's not possible," Veronica said.

"It's very possible," Stuart said. "To see him is to believe him. Can we have some discretion about this?"

"Of course," Veronica nodded. "No one would believe me anyway. I didn't believe Eve."

She sat down in the chair Stuart had vacated and placed the food on the desk.

"Have a nice lunch," Stuart smiled, "Winter and I have some things to sort out."

"Wait a minute," Winter said, "Mrs. Blair, you are a

barrister, aren't you?"

"Just a plain old lawyer," Veronica said.

"Can you review my trustee agreement and give me some advice? Stuart will pay you a retainer's fee."

"That is not my specialty," Veronica said, "but I used to work in wills and trusts eons ago. I can look it over."

"Good," Winter smiled. "Thank you. I am almost done with writing it. I hope we will become better acquainted. I want to marry your daughter."

"I am speechless," Veronica said when they exited the room. "No, not speechless; I am shocked."

Eve chuckled. "I told you so."

"You did," Veronica said. "Tell me everything from the beginning, and don't leave a thing out. How did he get here? Are you sure this is not just a big con?"

"Let me get my food," Eve said, rustling in the bag. "And then I'll spill it all."

She told her mother everything, from meeting him to his marriage proposal. "I love him, Mom," Eve said. "I can't describe it. The world suddenly made sense when I first saw him, like everything fell into place. He's kind, thoughtful, and so incredibly genuine. I know it might seem sudden, but it feels right, Mom. I've never been sure about anything in my life. And before you say it, I never felt this way about David. Not even a little bit. This is it. The real thing."

"And that's what gives me pause about it," Veronica said, putting down her fork. "He is a white man from a different time. A time when they had us as slaves."

Eve nodded. "He never had slaves. That's well documented."

"You are just setting yourself up for heartache. If he disappears in 1721, you'll be heartbroken, moping around the place like a lost sheep. I cannot believe you'd willingly put yourself through that again."

"Was he serious about wanting to marry you?" Veronica asked.

"Yes," Eve said. "But I am not so sure that I want to be rushed. This time, I want it to be forever."

"Good girl," Veronica said. "Does he truly make you happy?"

"He does," Eve said. "It's as if all the puzzle pieces have fallen into place. I didn't know I needed him until he appeared in my life. We might belong to different centuries, but I feel as if he knows what I'm thinking before I even say it."

"Well, that's good enough for me."

****

Stuart and Winter tried to retreat to the library, but the bridal party—a group of seven ladies in dresses somewhat similar to those worn by women in his century—tight bodices, full skirts, and side hoops to widen the hips—were standing in front of his portrait. Two photographers with lighting equipment and other paraphernalia were taking pictures.

The bride-to-be screamed and pointed at him, "Oh my God. Did anyone ever tell you that you look just like the man in the portrait behind us?"

Winter nodded. "I've heard that several times, Ma'am."

"You even talk like you're from the eighteenth century! Can I have a picture?" she asked.

"What's a picture?" Winter feigned ignorance.

"Oh my word, he doesn't know what a picture is, how authentic is this. In our century, it's like a portrait, just instant."

Winter chuckled. "I'd be much obliged."

"What's your name?" the bride-to-be asked.

"Winter Wesson. What's yours?"

"Ashley Roxborough. My husband and I are history teachers. We thought we would live it up Bridgerton style. And these are my six bridesmaids."

"What's Bridgerton style?" Winter frowned.

They all chuckled.

"It's a regency-style show on television," Stuart whispered behind him.

"Oh, I see," Winter nodded. "I am familiar with your television. I can't decide what to watch; everything is so interesting."

"Where are you from?" one lady asked. She had a British accent.

"Wessex," Winter answered.

He was relieved when she nodded. At least Wessex was still around.

He took two pictures with the women, and Stuart extricated him from them.

"Ladies, so sorry, but Mr. Wesson and I have an urgent meeting."

"I understand why Eve doesn't want me to come out while tours are going on unless I am conducting one myself," Winter said when they reached the owner's cottage. "I also understand why she wouldn't want to live here when we are married."

"Are you serious about marriage to Eve?" Stuart cleared his throat. "I mean, in this century, you don't have to get married to have sex. There are several methods of contraception for both men and women. Don't you want to play the field, see who else is around?" Stuart asked.

"No," Winter frowned. "Eve and I have a soul connection. I would like to honor that. Besides, I once married for business; this time, I want to marry for love. That's what I like about this century."

"A soul connection," Stuart shook his head.

"Are you married?" Winter asked.

"At the moment," Stuart sighed, "I don't know how long it will last. We are drifting apart. I long for my single days."

Winter smiled. "You do not sound unlike Walker; our father cannot get him to marry anyone. Whenever my father finds a suitable woman, he flees the country and goes on an adventure."

Stuart chuckled. "I can't believe I am here talking to you like this."

"You'll get used to it," Winter said.

"The first order of business we need to discuss is your new identity."

"My new identity," Winter whispered.

"Yes," Stuart said. "My predecessor, Rhona Wesson, found you an identity. We have been maintaining this identity for years."

"I am unclear as to what you mean," Winter said.

"Well, in the trustee agreement, you said we should prepare for you to integrate into this society. Having identification is key to that. Birth certificates were not required until much later in the nineteenth century. To live here, you have to have one. So Rhona took care of it. You now have a fully established identity with all the necessary documentation—a birth certificate, national insurance number, driver's license, etc. You have a complete background that aligns with your new persona."

"Your name is still Winter Wesson; you were born in Wesson County, Wessex, and your birthplace remains the same. Your parents are Claire and Robert Wesson. Their actual baby was stillborn. He would be thirty-two this year, so you are off by a few months. However, that's good enough. Robert is a descendant of Arthur. Your story is as close to the truth as possible. You've been living in Jamaica for the past couple of years, where you have been giving guest lectures about the early eighteenth century and writing books."

Winter laughed. "I see. I am a historian."

"That's right," Stuart nodded. "I'll bring your documents by tomorrow."

"The more you talk, the more ideas I have for the trustee agreement," Winter said. "I have been fortunate to have good descendants."

"You have been," Stuart nodded. "Your fortune has grown. I will give you a full financial report tomorrow. Unfortunately, you won't be able to see the properties in our portfolio, but we have weathered the storm through the years. You bought strategic properties in every parish in Jamaica."

"Of course, it has been a running joke that you bought it like you knew the future."

"Show me a map of the present and one of the past, and tell me what I bought," Winter said.

"Your wish is my command," Stuart nodded approvingly.

"I should also tell you that Isaac Stein booked a flight to get here; he is anxious to meet you. He called me when he got my message that you are here. He was in Egypt at an ancient library site; he said he found out more about the sundial."

"Really?" Winter asked.

Stuart nodded. "I can't wait to hear what he has to say."

Chapter Eighteen

Isaac Stein showed up on Friday evening after the great house was closed to visitors. Eve, Winter, Stuart, and Maud were having dinner on the owner's cottage veranda. They were almost done when Willie carried Stein around to meet them.

"I booked a place at Crimson Rest and had a nap," Isaac said in response to their greeting. "I just could not keep up anymore. I barely slept a wink since I got the message from Stuart." He stared at Winter; his eyes hardly strayed from him since his arrival, even after he sat down and nearly downed the whole pitcher of lemonade. "I came straight here. I can hardly believe this; time travel is possible. What I wouldn't do to study your brain."

Eve and Maud gasped. Stuart widened his eyes. "I thought you were an archaeologist, not a neurosurgeon."

"I am an archaeologist, but I discovered some fascinating things about how the sundial works. It works in tandem with the brain of the person who activated it. I imagine all of the magnetite crystals in Winter's brain are lit up like a Christmas tree the moment he activated the sundial. The magnetite crystals in the instrument and his brain are acting as one. He and the sundial are creating the reality we are all sharing now."

"When I walked into the great house, my gradiometer, the instrument we use to measure magnetic fields, went haywire. This place feels different. The instrument didn't have to go crazy for me to feel it."

"I know what you mean," Eve said. "Everybody says it when they come here."

"It feels like the site I am at in Egypt," Stein said. "There is almost something otherworldly about it. I am surprised that more phenomena haven't occurred up here."

"Strange things happen up here all the time," Maud said. "Willie and I just don't talk about it. For instance, I can travel in time, too. It usually occurs while I am sleeping but just like Winter, I cannot leave the great house."

"Ah," Dr. Stein nodded. "That is no surprise. The magnetite crystals create a powerful magnetic field, especially at certain times of the year."

"And when people leave here, they don't remember that they met Winter," Willie added, speaking up for the first time. He usually left the talking to Maud.

"Magnetite crystals?" Maud asked. "What's that?"

"They are crystals in the human brain that play a key role in how we perceive things and store information," Isaac explained. "Ancient people knew about them and how to manipulate them to time travel. There is much we do not know about how it works. It's not until recently that scientists have taken seriously, the theory that we have crystals in the brain. This type of talk was called pseudoscience, but lo and behold, I dug up ancient manuscripts that freely talk about magnetite crystals in our brain."

"The people in this century think we are more advanced than those who came before, but I have a theory that this world goes through resets, and after every reset, mankind starts all over, and significant technologies are lost. What I wouldn't do to get my hands on the tech that built the pyramids at Giza or the ancient knowledge that allowed civilizations like the Mayans to predict astronomical events with such precision," Stein mused, his eyes flickering with excitement. "But alas, we're left piecing together fragments, trying to unlock the secrets of our ancestors."

"So, have you found anything new about the usage of the sundial? Is it responsible for making Winter disappear?" Eve asked anxiously.

"He disappeared from the eighteenth century," Dr. Stein said, "but that doesn't mean he disappeared from this century. I think he made a choice to stay here."

Winter nodded. "That makes sense."

"You can wear out the magnetite crystals in your brain from traveling frequently. It takes a lot of power to time travel. When the crystals are burnt out, you will cease to function. You may end up a vegetable or dead."

"How many times is too many times?" Stuart asked.

"I have no clue," Dr. Stein admitted.

"This is my fourth time here," Winter said.

"I want to see it," Dr. Stein stood up. "I want to put my hand on it."

They all got up and went with him to the sundial. They waited around while he took pictures and asked questions.

"This is a fine example of ancient technology," he said, standing over the sundial and looking down at it in the waning sun. "It accounted for everything. It allows the user to move between times but doesn't allow you to go to a timeline where you have been before. And it contains its power within a specific area so that you cannot pollute a timeline, and where it is deactivated, it purges the timeline."

"How can it be deactivated though?" Winter asked.

"It has to be removed."

"But not before I return and set my life in order."

"Good, just tell me when you are ready to do so. If you would be willing to part with it, my university would buy it from you. We'd love to study it."

"After my next travel," Winter said. "I'll consider giving it to you for science. I want to see beyond these gates and what the twenty-first century has to offer."

"A word of caution," Dr. Stein said, "no one will remember who you are when it leaves here. The events leading up to your traveling, everything will be wiped clean. You will have to renew and restart relationships; all the memories of your past will be purged. Only you will remember."

Eve and Winter's eyes collided.

"That can't be true," Eve whispered.

"It can be," Dr. Stein said. That's what I wanted to share. The document I found plainly states that time traveling is localized for a reason, so the purging can be localized, too."

"So, no one will remember me?" Winter asked.

"That's right," Dr. Stein nodded.

"So, all the conversations and emotions..." Winter looked at Eve, "will be forgotten?"

"Yes, from this century," Stein nodded. "Think it over carefully before you decide."

Winter winced. "What about love? Will Eve still love me?"

Dr. Stein considered the question, "I didn't read this, in any ancient text, I am just going off speculation, but I have found that true love transcends time and memory. If your connection with Eve is genuine and profound, it may endure even in the face of such circumstances. Love, after all, is more than just memories; it's the bond that exists between two souls."

****

"I'll never forget you," Eve said, as they snuggled together on the veranda chairs and watched the stars.

"You will," Winter said. "What's the use of coming back if the woman you came back for doesn't know you."

"Then make me fall in love with you again," Eve said. "It wasn't hard the first time. I fell for you in less than a week."

"You'll laugh when I tell you the truth," Winter said. "I'll have to convince you that I am Winter Wesson from the past."

"So convince me," Eve said.

Chapter Nineteen

Traveling was more challenging this time around. He had loads of things to remember to do. He had property to buy, a trust agreement to construct from memory, and a life to give up. Most of his affairs were entrusted to Wesley. And even though Winter knew he was up to the task, seeing his young brother trying to absorb everything he was reminding him to do made him doubt himself.

"I am up to the task, Winter," Wesley said optimistically.

"The trust agreement is not complicated. I'll be in charge of your trust till my dying day. I will follow your instructions to the letter, and I will ensure that my successor does the same and so on. If I could live in another century, I would do it too, especially one more advanced than ours," Wesley assured him. "Don't be sad about leaving."

Walker was more morose. "I will miss you, brother."

"I would have had to return to England after Willhelm dies," Winter said. "Our adventures together would be over anyway."

"Yes, I know," Walker said. "A little of what I feel is envy. You get to live out your life with a totally different adventure. Never forget me."

"Never," Winter promised.

He waited for the equinox and went to the sundial again. It was bittersweet, but Eve was waiting for him.

And there she was, sitting anxiously at the front steps of the great house, with Maud, Stuart, and Dr. Stein beside her.

She ran toward him to hug him, and he held her tight.

"It was a long, hard three months," Eve said into his neck. "I missed you so much. I am happy you are back."

"I feel the same," Winter said.

"I don't want to wait to see the other side," he said to Dr. Stein. "You can remove the sundial whenever you are ready. Did you have the replica made, Stuart?"

Stuart nodded. "I did."

He planned to win back Eve and wanted to get it going fast.

"Then let's do it," Winter said.

"First thing tomorrow," Dr. Stein nodded. "I arranged to have it gone before anyone can tell we are installing a copy."

****

Winter woke up in the owner's cottage. The place seemed still. He glanced at the clock; it was almost nine. He had stayed up all night while Eve outlined a step-by-step guide to winning her back.

"Try to convince me like you did the last time, show me the hiding places, tell me your story, stare at me a while," Winter chuckled. "Stare at you?"

"Yes," Eve smiled. "There is something in your eyes that

pulls me in. It speaks to me, I can't avoid it. In the Winter's Eve poem, you say in my eyes, you see your home?"

Winter nodded.

"In your eyes, I see my destiny." Eve said.

"You do?" Winter whispered.

"I do," Eve said. "Removing the sundial will not change that. I will eventually remember us. You can also ensure I get those letters you used to write to me."

"Great minds think alike," Winter kissed her softly. "I already have that in my trust agreement. I had to address a letter to Stuart personally. I left him a list of things that I wanted him to do for me when I return."

Eve chuckled. "You are crafty."

"I also wrote Maud," Winter said. "I find that I don't want to lose her friendship. The three of you are my family."

He could hear a grass cutter in the distance. He got up, stretched, and looked outside. It was clear and pristine where he used to see the hazy blur, where he imagined the sea would be. The sundial was gone.

He hurriedly washed his face, brushed his teeth, and went around to the front of the house. He didn't even put on shoes. He could see across the street. He walked through the gate and over to the other side of the road and touched the growing plants there.

"Oh hey," a lady walked up the hill. "Good morning."

"Good morning," he said.

She smiled at him. "I have never seen anybody so happy to touch the grass."

Winter chuckled. "I have never been on this side before."

"I understand the awe, this is a picturesque hill," the lady nodded. "It's my first time in Crimson Hills too. I just arrived and had to take a walk. Do you know if the tours at the Great House are any good?"

"I heard it's splendid," Winter nodded.

"Well, I'll be back. Have a good day."

He was about to cross the road when a vehicle came toward him. It stopped.

The window wound down. It was Stuart.

He grinned. "Good morning, Stuart."

Stuart widened his eyes. "Winter Wesson?"

"That's me," he nodded.

"So, you arrived early," Stuart smiled. "Welcome to Crimson Hill Great House. We have a packed day ahead. You left me quite a list."

"So you got it?" Winter asked.

"I did," Stuart said. "You outlined what you needed to do every day. Today on your agenda, after your arrival is a tour of Rafferty House with Eve. I just went there to ensure the cleaners did a good job. You also said you want driving lessons and to go clothes shopping. You want to change your wardrobe."

"I do," Winter nodded.

"I hired a stylist," Stuart said, "he'll be here tomorrow. As for driving lessons, how soon do you want to start?"

"As soon as possible," Winter said.

"Well, I can arrange for a class today."

"Good," Winter nodded. "Thanks, Stuart."

"It's my job," Stuart smiled. "Do you want a lift back to the cottage?"

"No," Winter said. "I think I am fine. I was so excited to see the other side of the road clearly that I came out here to see it up close."

Stuart nodded. "Well then, see you shortly."

"Wait!" Winter said. "What's my story?"

"Your story?" Stuart asked, confused.

"My life story," Winter said. "As in, where am I from?

Who are my parents?"

"You were born in Wessex, England, to Claire and Robert Wesson. You are a history book author. It's your first time in Crimson Hills, and you were excited to come here to see where the original Winter Wesson lived. You instructed the board to buy Rafferty house; you wanted a place to stay nearby to write your first novel. You said it is based on a man from the eighteenth century falling in love with a woman in the twenty-first."

"I see," Winter nodded.

Stuart smiled. "Well, that's the story you want the rest of the world to hear, anyway. The trustee agreement had a special letter for me from 1721. I have always been a little freaked out by it. You outlined what happened before the sun dial was removed, your visits, our conversations, everything. You told me that I would forget everything when Dr. Stein took the sun dial away, but your notes were what would keep your memory alive."

"And you believed it?" Winter asked wonderingly.

"Of course, I do." Stuart frowned, "as the head of your trustee board, I had to, you left clear, and specific instructions for your return. It had to be real, nobody from the eighteenth century could know the things you know."

"What about Eve?" Winter asked. "Do you know if she remembers me?"

"She hasn't said a thing," Stuart said, "but she has been looking cheerful lately."

Winter inhaled. "I left her my diaries. I told Maud to give them to her, three months before my return.

"Well, if you told Maud to do it, she would do it." Stuart said.

"I feel nervous," Winter said.

"Why should you?" Stuart asked, "you left your time to be

with her. It's the greatest love story I've ever heard."

Stuart drove up the driveway, Winter followed slowly.

Chapter Twenty

"**M**om, I don't have a date for the gala," Eve told her mother. "Yes, it's the second year in a row. And no, I don't care how it looks."

"I'll be your date," a voice said across from her desk. She spun around, almost getting whiplash. "Excuse me, I didn't hear you come in," Eve said huskily. "Mom, I have to go."

"You," Eve whispered.

"Me," Winter nodded.

She hung up the phone and looked at the guy in front of her. "Winter Wesson, the original?"

"Yes," Winter chuckled. "Did you read the diaries?"

"Yes," Eve nodded. "It's a nice love story—a little unbelievable in parts. I don't appreciate you using my name or my family's name. And how did you know about David and his two-year issue with relationships? Are you his friend? Did Maud put you up to this?"

"No one put me up to this," Winter sputtered.

"The question is, how did you know my name and so many specific details about me? Are you a stalker, Fake Winter?"

Winter laughed. He couldn't help it. "You did tell me it was going to be rough trying to convince you that any of this happened."

Eve leaned back in her chair. "Don't get me wrong, it's a nice story, but I know who you are. You are Winter Theodore Wesson. It's your first time in Crimson Hills. You want a tour of Rafferty House, where you will stay to write your historical fiction book about a girl who lived in the twenty-first century and a guy who came from the eighteenth century through time travel. You are somehow using me as your muse."

Winter smiled. "You said I should show you all the hiding places around the house, including where I hide the whisky and the secret compartment in the desk where I sent you notes from the eighteenth century."

"What are you talking about?" Eve frowned.

"Let's go," Winter said.

"Where are we going?" Eve asked.

"First, we go to the kitchens. I'll show you my whisky stash."

Eve got up. She wore black jeans that hugged her curvy figure and a polo shirt with the Crimson Hill Great House logo on the front.

He smiled. He would never get tired of seeing this woman. That was something that he knew deep down.

They walked to the kitchen.

"We should go to Rafferty House for the tour," Eve said. "I blocked out my morning for that. Stuart said…"

"I know, we'll tour Rafferty House," Winter said, entering the kitchen, "but I need to jog your memory a bit."

He went above the oven and started removing the brick.

Eve was impressed when he withdrew the bottle of whisky.

"Would you like a drink, my lady?" he asked.

"Hell no, it's too early to drink." Eve frowned. "And that whisky can't be good if it's three hundred years old."

"Maybe older, Winter said, "whisky can last for centuries if stored properly. We'll save it for later. I want to show you something."

"What?" Eve asked.

"In the counting house, the desk holds a letter I wrote to you. It is for your eyes only."

They went to the counting house. Eve stood while he fiddled with the latch on the desk. The letter was still there. He breathed a sigh of relief.

Eve gasped. "How did you know it was there?"

"I wrote it to you from 1721," Winter said. "I want you to read it today, now."

Eve took the letter from him gingerly.

"You are handsome and crazy," she said, half in disbelief. Winter laughed.

She opened the letter and read the first line, "My dearest Eve Lyn Blair."

When she read that, she looked up at him and down at the paper. "What is this?"

"A letter from the eighteenth century," Winter replied.

"My story is a long one. It begins with me acquiring Hezekiah's sundial. I activated it and moved forward in time, three hundred years. After my third trip, I saw you. You were going to attend a gala," she read aloud.

Eve looked up at him and gasped. "Is this for real?"

"It is," Winter said.

Eve sat down abruptly and started reading. Her eyes welled with tears as he described the events leading up to the removal of the sundial.

"I had no idea..." she whispered, her voice trembling. "Why don't I remember?"

"Nobody does," Winter said. "A side effect of removing the sundial is that everything is forgotten. Only the time traveler remembers. But I don't want to be alone in this. I returned to be with you, and I am ready for this adventure together. The sundial can erase many things, but it cannot erase true love.

"I know it's a lot to take in," Winter said. "I don't want to overwhelm you too much. I know you must have loads of questions."

"I do," Eve nodded. "So many questions."

"I hope this poem helps," Winter said, handing her a piece of paper that said, 'Winter's Eve.'

"You are mine, and I am yours,
You are Winter's Eve,
I would defy the hands of time and, in your love, believe.
For in your eyes, I see my home,
A haven pure and true,
With every breath, I am drawn to you,
So let the seasons come and go,
In your arms, I'll find reprieve,
For you are mine, and I am yours,
Together, we'll never leave."

"Look into my eyes Eve," Winter said, "we discussed this before, and you said in my eyes you see your destiny."

Eve looked into his dark green eyes; past memories flooded her thoughts, disjointed and broken at first and then slowly piecing themselves together like a puzzle. She felt a warmth in her heart, a familiarity transcending time.

"Winter's Eve," she whispered, a smile tugging at the

corners of her lips. "I remember now. I remember us."

Winter's gaze softened, relief washing over him like a gentle wave. "You do?"

Eve nodded tears of recognition shimmering in her eyes. "Yes, I remember our love, our first meeting... everything."

Winter pulled her into his embrace, holding her close as if afraid she might slip away again. "I never lost hope that you would remember," he murmured against her hair. "And now that you do, we can face whatever challenges lie ahead together."

Eve nodded, burying her face in the crook of his neck, feeling the steady beat of his heart against her cheek. "Together," she echoed, her voice filled with newfound determination. "Forever and always."

Epilogue

Seven Years Later

This year, her mother's gala was being held on the grounds of the great house. Maud had offered to babysit, and the children would stay with her overnight in the carriage house.

"Don't worry, Miss Eve, Wesley and Summer are angels compared to my two grandchildren," Maud reassured.

"Besides, I have been reading their father's diaries to them. They love his adventures," she added.

Eve smiled, "Between you and Winter, my children will grow up confused."

She kissed the children goodnight. "Be good for your Aunt Maud."

"Daddy! Daddy!" Summer and Wesley yelled as if they hadn't just seen their father at home at Rafferty House where they lived.

Winter appeared at the door in his tux, his hair neatly combed, looking for all the world like a hunky Superman. Eve smiled as Winter knelt down to them, his eyes sparkling.

"Yes, my loves?" he said, his voice gentle.

"Daddy, will you tell us a story before you go to the party?" Summer's eyes lit up with excitement.

"Yes, Daddy," Wesley said, "tell us about pirates."

"No, Daddy, can we hear about the one where the adventurer crosses time to be with his lady?" Summer pouted.

Winter glanced at Eve and grinned. "I am partial to both of those."

"Just one story," Eve warned. "We are hosting the gala; we need to be present." She headed to the door.

"Once upon a time, an adventurer set sail across the seas on a quest. He wanted to discover new lands and treasures beyond imagination," Winter began, his voice carrying a hint of adventure. "In his journeys, he encountered a man who sold him a sundial. The sundial was a time machine."

Summer and Wesley leaned in, captivated by their father's words as if they hadn't heard the story a thousand times.

"He turned the sundial two hundred degrees and found himself in a world unlike any he had ever known," Winter continued, his eyes glinting excitedly. "There, he met a lady whose beauty and spirit enchanted him beyond measure."

"Were there pirates in this world, Daddy?" Wesley interrupted eagerly.

Winter chuckled softly. "Ah, no, my boy, the pirates were in the world the man was coming from, and they were no match for the bravery of our adventurer."

Summer sighed dreamily. "And did he stay with the lady forever?"

"Well," Winter said with a grin, "not immediately. But one thing's for certain—no matter where his adventures took him or what century he was in, his heart always found its way back to her."

Eve smiled as she listened from the doorway, her heart swelling with love for her family.

The End

Dear Reader,

This is it, the Winter Wesson story. I enjoyed writing this one. Thank you for joining me on this adventure. I hope Winter's tale brought you as much joy in reading as it has brought me in writing.

Keep reading for an excerpt of Cinnamon, the first book in the Spice and Stone stories.

If you have comments or suggestions, I welcome them. You can reach me and receive a reply at brenalbar@gmail.com.

Thanks again. All the best,

Brenda

Excerpt: Cinnamon Book 1- Spice and Stone Series

Cinnamon entered the hairdressing parlor and spa where her sister worked and tried to sit unobtrusively in the stylish waiting room. She would probably wait for Cayenne for a while; it was a little after five, and they had agreed to meet at five-thirty. It was her birthday, and they were going to celebrate, but she didn't mind the wait.

The waiting area was like a hotel lounge; the chairs were comfortable, the smell there was amazing and soft jazz music played in the background, creating a serene atmosphere. She would flip through some magazines, see the latest hair trends and spa treatments, and covertly watch the customers come and go. You had to have money to afford Lookbook Hair and Spa's services.

They were a full-service beauty place owned and operated by Tony Ray, who was famous as a stylist to local celebrities and a few international ones. After being on her own for two years, her sister had been over the moon happy to get her own station at this particular salon. She made more money here, met many influential people, and was usually the first to hear when juicy stories broke nationally.

Unfortunately for them, their mother, Anise Crystal, was dominating the current news cycle again. Even today's local newspapers, displayed on the magazine rack beside her, had as the headline: "Former Escort Anise Crystal says she deserves every penny she inherited from the late Senator Richard Greystone. His wife, Noreen Greystone, says not so fast!"

Cinnamon read the first couple of paragraphs:

The war between the late Richard Greystone's family, owners of the Caribbean's leading wine company, Greystone Wines, and Anise Crystal, known for her relationships with high-profile men and who had in the past dabbled with prostitution, has escalated. Noreen Greystone, determined to protect her family's legacy and the reputation of Greystone Wines, hastily organized a press conference at the vineyard estate. Standing before a backdrop adorned with the vineyard's iconic spice and stone logo, she addressed the media with poise and frustration.

"As the wife of the late Senator Richard Greystone and co-owner of Greystone Wines, I was blindsided by my husband's will. I am not disputing how he wanted to disburse his personal wealth; it was his to do with as he pleased. But leaving shares in our family business to Anise Crystal is a slap in the face to everything we've built together," Noreen declared, her voice unwavering. "Greystone Wines has been a labor of love, a testament to the dedication and passion that our family has poured into it for generations. To see it potentially tainted by associations that run contrary to the values we hold dear is both distressing and unacceptable.

"The family's legal team will be challenging the validity of the contested bequest. We vow to protect the interests of Greystone Wines and its stakeholders, ensuring that the vineyard will continue to thrive with the same excellence it has always been known for."

In the meantime, Anise Crystal has responded to Noreen's press conference with a sly wink and her signature sultry smile.

"Richard has his reasons for giving me equal shares as his sons in the family business. I intend to honor his generosity by accepting those shares. I have run a business selling wigs for years; it is reputable and profitable. I resent the inferences that Noreen Greystone is making about me, that I am somehow not worthy.

"I say, bring on the lawyers, grandma. I have my own lawyers, too."

Cinnamon grimaced. She didn't need to read further. At that point, Anise was taunting the family.

Admittedly, it was all salacious and juicy; speculations ran rife as to why the Senator would leave most of his personal wealth to a non-family member and, worst of all, to Anise, a woman who had admitted publicly to doing sex work when she was barely in her teenage years.

That, too, had been a recent interview where Anise had told snippets of her life story, stuff that Cinnamon and her sisters hadn't heard before.

"I did sex work at the tender age of thirteen. I needed to do it to survive after I ran away from home. It was a dark time in my life. No child should ever have to do that. I had customers who many would regard as standard bearers in this society. Let me tell you, there are freaks all over society, and you should not put anyone on a pedestal."

That interview had coincided with Richard Greystone's death and revelation of the contents of his will. And suddenly, there were all sorts of theories floating around town. The chief one was that Richard Greystone had been a customer of Anise when she was a child prostitute and had left her his money and shares in his wine company to assuage his guilty conscience.

His reputation was taking a posthumous beating in the public sphere. His three sons and their children were catching heat for some of the speculations floating around. They couldn't grieve in peace. For some sections of society, they were guilty by association.

Everyone was shell-shocked, including her.

Discover Exclusive Offers and Be the First to Know!

If you haven't already, don't miss out on the opportunity to join my New Release Newsletter! Sign up today and become part of an exclusive community where you'll be among the first to hear about my latest book releases and take advantage of special prices.

Why join my mailing list?

Be the First: Get a head start and be the first to know when I release a new book.

Exclusive Discounts: Unlock special prices available only to subscribers. Enjoy limited time offers and save big on your favorite books.

Quick and Easy: Signing up takes less than 30 seconds.

To join, visit https://www.brenalbar.com/newsletter or scan the QR code below.

Thank you for your support, and happy reading!

Ridgeview Series

The Ridgeview series follows five couples on the Jamaican north coast in the luxurious community of Ridgeview. It explores their everyday struggles with careers, children, and family drama. Each book touches on love, marriage, and trust as the characters face challenges that test their relationships.

Ride or Die (Book 1)
Play For Keeps (Book 2)
Through Thick and Thin (Book 3)
Tried and True (Book 4)
Stay With You (Book 5)

Spice and Stone Series

Join three extraordinary girls—Cinnamon, Cayenne, and Sage—as they navigate the intricate flavors of life, love, and romance in the captivating Spice and Stone series.

Cinnamon (Book 1)
Cayenne (Book 2)
Sage (Book3)

The Crimson Hill Series

Where family drama, romance, and a touch of sci-fi blend seamlessly in the enchanting backdrop of a small town in Jamaica. Prepare to embark on an unforgettable journey as secrets unravel, passions ignite, and destinies intertwine.

No Goodbye (Book 1)
No Misunderstanding (Book 2)
No Ordinary Love (Book 3)
No Fairy Tale (Book 4)
No Letting Go (Book 5)
No Strings Attached (Book 6)
No More Mrs. Nice Girl (Book 7)
No Place Like You (Book 8)
Knight and Day (Book 8.5)
No Expectations (Book 9)
Ice and Fyre (Book 9.5)
No Surrender (Book 10)
No Time for Love (Book 11)
No Promises (Book 12)
Winter's Eve (Book 13)

The Wiley Brothers

Step into the world of the Wiley Brothers, where tragedy weaves an unbreakable bond and love becomes their guiding light. In this captivating series, follow the journey of six remarkable boys as they navigate the tumultuous path of growing up without parents, discovering love, and finding their place in a challenging world.

Between Brothers (Book 0)- How it all began…
For Pete's Sake (Book 1)- Preston's story.
Crossing Jordan (Book 2)-Jordan's story.
Fire and Walter (Book 3)- Walter's story.
The Perfect Guy (Book 4)-Guy's Story.
The Patience of a Saint (Book 5)- Saint's Story.
A Case of Love (Book 6)- Case's Story.

The Pryce Sisters

Follow the remarkable journey of the Pryce triplets as they navigate the complexities of growing up, discovering romance, and embracing the exhilarating challenges of the new adult years.

Baby For A Pryce- Book 1
Right Pryce Wrong Time – Book 2
Yours, For A Pryce- Book 3

The Jacksons

Prepare to be enthralled by the captivating saga of the Jackson family. In this gripping series, secrets unravel, paternity questions loom, and love blooms in the most unexpected corners.

Ace- Book 1
Deuce- Book 2
Trey- Book 3
Quade- Book 4

The Scarlett Series

Their patriarch died and unexpectedly left each of them a fortune. Watch as the Scarlett family navigate their way through the ups and downs of sudden wealth, family secrets, and the complicated dynamics of their relationships.

Scarlett Baby (Book 1)
Scarlett Sinner (Book 2)
Scarlett Secret (Book 3)
Scarlett Love (Book 4)
Scarlett Promise (Book 5)
Scarlett Bride (Book 6)
Scarlett Heart (Book 7)

Magnolia Sisters

They were the rejects. The worst of the lot, they grew up in a girl's home together and formed sisterly bonds. Each book in the series tells the story of a different girl and the unique struggles and triumphs she faces along the way. With themes of friendship, forgiveness, and the power of love, the "Magnolia Sisters" series is a heartwarming and inspiring read that you won't want to put down.

Dear Mystery Guy- Book 1
Bad Girl Blues- Book 2
Her Mistaken Dream- Book 3
Just Like Yesterday – Book 4

New Song Series

A group of friends started out as a church band, see how each of them navigate their personal and professional lives while staying true to their faith and facing challenges along the way. With themes of forgiveness, redemption, and second chances, the New Song Series is a captivating read for anyone who enjoys heartwarming stories of love and faith.

Going Solo- Book 1
Duet on Fire- Book 2
Tangled Chords- Book 3
Broken Harmony- Book 4
A Past Refrain- Book 5
Perfect Melody- Book 6

The Bancrofts

The Bancroft family delves into the inner workings of academia and the high-stakes world of university politics. The family wrestles with the pressures of maintaining their family's legacy, they must confront their own demons and navigate the complex relationships that bind them together. From unexpected love affairs and betrayals to scandals and secrets that threaten to tear them apart, this is a series that will keep you captivated until the very end.

Homely Girl- Book 0
Saving Face- Book 1
Tattered Tiara- Book 2
Private Dancer- Book 3
Goodbye Lonely- Book 4
Practice Run- Book 5
Sense of Rumor- Book 6
A Younger Man- Book 7
Just To See Her- Book 8

Three Rivers Series

Three Rivers Series, a captivating tale of love, redemption, and second chances set in a picturesque community in St. Ann's Bay, Jamaica.

Private Sins- Book 1
Loving Mr. Wright- Book 2
Unholy Matrimony- Book 3
If It Ain't Broke- Book 4

The Resetter Series

The Resetter Series takes a look at a rare kind of person, a person who can travel back in time, but they only have one chance to get things right if they go back! With themes of second chances, changing the past and the power of love, the resetters series is a captivating time travel romance that many readers have described as a page turner.

Never Too Late- Book 1
Never Say Never- Book 2
Now or Never- Book 3
Almost Never- Book 4

On the Rebound Series

Experience the gripping and emotionally charged On the Rebound series, where love, betrayal, and redemption collide in a whirlwind of passion and secrets. Brace yourself for a journey filled with drama, cheating scandals, DNA questions, and ultimately, the power of second chances and finding love again.

On the Rebound- Book 1
On the Rebound Book 2

Standalone Books

Full Circle- After graduating from university, Diana wanted to return to Jamaica to find her siblings. What she didn't foresee was that she would meet Robert Cassidy and that both their pasts would be intertwined, and that disturbing questions would pop up about their parentage just when they were getting close.

After the End- Torn between two lovers. Colleen married her high school sweetheart, Isaiah, hoping that they would live happily ever after, but life intruded, and Isaiah disappeared at sea. She found work with the rich and handsome Enrique Lopez as a housekeeper and realized that she couldn't keep him at arm's length.

Love Triangle: Three Sides to the Story- George, the husband. Marie, the wife, and Karen-the mistress. They all get to tell their side of the story.

New Beginnings- Inner-city girl Geneva was offered an opportunity of a lifetime when she learned that her 'real' father was a wealthy man. Her decision to live up-town meant she had to leave Froggie, her 'ghetto don,' behind. She also found herself battling with her stepmother and battling her emotions for Justin, a suave up-towner.

The Preacher and the Prostitute- Prostitution and the clergy don't mix. Tell that to ex-prostitute Maribel, who finds herself in love with the Pastor at her church. Can an ex-prostitute and a pastor have a future together?

Historical Fiction

You won't want to miss out on these two captivating reads!

"The Pull of Freedom" tells the story of a slave family and their desperate struggle for freedom in Jamaica's colonial era. Follow the journey of these brave individuals as they fight for their right to be free, facing danger, heartbreak, and unimaginable obstacles along the way.

"The Empty Hammock" takes readers on a journey through time, as a modern woman finds herself transported back to the Taino era of Jamaica's history. Experience the wonder and mystery of this ancient culture through her eyes, as she learns about their traditions, beliefs, and way of life. With richly drawn characters and a beautifully realized setting, "The Empty Hammock" is a must-read for anyone who loves historical fiction that transports them to another time and place.

Short Story Collections

Di Taxi Ride and Other Stories- Funny stories about Jamaican life to make you laugh.

9 789769 743007